KT-464-650

Luke's eyes had darkened, and he stared at her mouth with such fascination it made things inside her heat up then melt down.

Keira gulped and tried to remember the friends thing. And that this was a *rational* time of day. She tried to focus on what they'd been talking about.

'You should really do something special for Jason for Christmas, you know. All kids need Christmas—even teenagers.' Instinct told her Luke needed it too. 'There's a magic to Christmas you can't get at any other time of year.'

She recognised the precise moment his gaze shifted to her legs. It was as if he'd reached out and stroked her with one lean, tanned finger. A quiver ran through her. Her breathing sped up. So did his. Her nerves drew tauter, tighter, until she thought they'd catapult her into something she'd regret.

It would be something Luke would definitely regret.

CHRISTMAS AT CANDLEBARK FARM

BY
MICHELLE DOUGLAS

First published in Great Britain 2010
Harlequin Mills & Boon Limited,
Eton House, 18-24 Paradise Road, Richmond, Surrey TW9 1SR

© Michelle Douglas 2010

ISBN: 978 0 263 21558 8

Harlequin Mills & Boon policy is to use papers that are natural, renewable and recyclable products and made from wood grown in sustainable forests. The logging and manufacturing process conform to the legal environmental regulations of the country of origin.

Printed and bound in Great Britain
by CPI Antony Rowe, Chippenham, Wiltshire

At the age of eight **Michelle Douglas** was asked what she wanted to be when she grew up. She answered, 'A writer.' Years later she read an article about romance-writing and thought, *Ooh, that'll be fun.* She was right.

When she's not writing she can usually be found with her nose buried in a book. She is currently enrolled in an English Masters programme for the sole purpose of indulging her reading and writing habits further. She lives in a leafy suburb of Newcastle, on Australia's east coast, with her own romantic hero—husband Greg, who is the inspiration behind all her happy endings. Michelle would love you to visit her at her website, www.michelledouglas.com

To Cate, and all our memories of the pink flat

CHAPTER ONE

KEIRA KEELY climbed out of her car and pushed her sunglasses up to rest on the top of her head before double-checking the written instructions the estate agency had given her.

Since she'd turned off the highway several kilometres back she'd travelled along this gravel lane for precisely six and a quarter minutes, just as the receptionist at the real estate agency had told her to.

This had to be the place. She hadn't passed a single house on the road so far, and there wasn't another house in sight. This had to be it—Candlebark Farm.

She hoped so. The big old homestead with its wide shady verandas looked inviting in the December sunshine, and after six hours on the road inviting was exactly what she needed. The country township of Gunnedah was a far cry from the hustle and bustle of Sydney, but so far it hadn't lived up to its promise of easygoing country hospitality.

She stretched her arms above her head and shook out her legs, did her best to banish her irritation.

'Some old-fashioned country hospitality is exactly what we need, Munchkin.' She patted her still-flat tummy. 'And, believe me, this place looks like it delivers that in spades.'

She pushed through the front gate. The lawn was a little long and the shrubs a little shrubby, but that only added to the charm of the place. She paused, breathed in the country goodness, and willed some of its peace to enter her soul.

The day had proved a complete shambles so far. Not only had the estate agent not been free to take her through her aunt's house—although when she'd rung him during the week he'd assured her it wouldn't be a problem—but her appointment with her aunt's solicitor had been cancelled too. 'We can reschedule it for Wednesday, Ms Keely.'

Wednesday! It was Saturday. She was only here for a week. With tight lips the secretary had pencilled Keira in for Tuesday morning for a 'short' appointment. Whatever *that* meant. Keira reminded herself the cancellation hadn't been the secretary's fault.

Her platform sandals with their pink, lime and aqua straps—super-comfortable and strangely accommodating of the way her feet had started to swell—clattered against the wood of the veranda. They were so noisy she half expected to find someone waiting for her at the front door by the time she reached it.

But no.

She tried the old-fashioned knocker and waited. Knocked again. And waited some more.

She glanced back at her car. She had groceries that would spoil soon if she didn't get them out of the heat. Had the Hilliers—the family who lived at Candlebark—forgotten she was coming?

She followed the veranda around to the back of the house. 'Hello?'

After a moment the back screen door jerked open. A boy stared out at her—a teenage boy, wearing a scowl. Keira swallowed. 'Um…is this Candlebark Farm?'

'Yeah.'

She pointed back the way she'd come. 'You didn't hear me knocking on the front door?'

The scowl deepened. 'No one uses the front.'

Right. She'd remember that for future reference.

She drew in a breath and had opened her mouth, meaning

to introduce herself, when the boy muttered, 'If you're looking for my dad he's in the barn.' With that he disappeared back inside the house, the screen door clattering shut after him.

Keira blinked. Right. The, um…barn.

Shading her eyes, she surveyed the landscape spread before her. Just beyond the fence line, stretching for as far as the eye could see, waist-high stalks nodded and swayed, making intriguing patterns as the breeze travelled through them, their golden heads bouncing and jostling. Wheat. Unsurprising, she told herself. After all, Gunnedah was smack-bang in the middle of New South Wale's wheat belt. And although it made a fine sight—pretty, even—she hadn't travelled six hours to admire wheat fields.

She turned her attention to the array of outbuildings on her left. Without further ado she set off towards the largest one.

Were all teenagers surly?

'Ooh, Munchkin, we're going to have some serious talks before you hit that age.'

The thought of the baby nestled safely inside her made Keira's chest expand. She flung her arms out, as if to hug the world, and lifted her face skywards to relish the warmth of the sun. A laugh escaped her. So what if there were a few hiccups this week? That was what she was here to sort out.

Just like that, her usual optimism reasserted itself. She chuckled again, and admitted maybe that had more to do with the fact that her nausea had receded. Finally.

The barn's double doors stood wide open. 'Hello?' She stepped inside. It took her eyes a moment to adjust to the sudden dimness. No sound but her own disturbed the quiet. She moved further inside and made her voice louder. 'Hello?'

'There's no need to shout.'

She nearly jumped out of her skin when a man, flat on his back on some kind of trolley, emerged from beneath a tractor almost directly in front of her. She backed up a few steps to give him more room. He had grease on one cheek and both hands. He didn't get up. His scowl, identical to the teenage boy's back at the house, proclaimed their kinship.

'You lost? Look—head back the way you came. When you hit the sealed road turn left and go straight ahead. Gunnedah is about fifteen minutes away.'

He slid back under the tractor again. She swore she heard him add in an undertone, 'Where you can buy a map.'

Ten minutes ago she might well have been tempted to kick him—not literally, of course. Now the misunderstanding only made her laugh. 'This is Candlebark Farm, isn't it? If so, then I'm not lost. Are you Mr Hillier?'

With a long-suffering sigh he emerged again. 'Yeah? So? Who wants to know?'

'I'm Keira Keely.'

He didn't sit up, so she rested her hands on her knees and grinned down at him. 'I'm renting your room for the next week.'

Those dark eyes blinked. The face shuttered closed, but the frown deepened, carving deep grooves either side of his mouth. Keira's renewed optimism wavered. It wasn't the kind of mouth that promised country hospitality.

'You sure you're meant to arrive today?'

'A hundred percent certain.'

'Right.' In one fluid motion he was on his feet and wiping his hands on a rag that hung from the back of his jeans. 'Didn't Jason show you your room?'

The surly teenager?

The man still hadn't cracked a smile. She swallowed. He was tall, lean-hipped and broad-shouldered. She hadn't noticed that when he'd been sprawled at her feet. He was glaring too. And his words sounded like an accusation.

It hit her then how quiet it was out here...how isolated. She took a step back.

'You—uh—' he lifted a hand in her direction and made as if to grab her '—might want to watch—'

She took another hasty step back, her sandal-clad foot landing in an oozing, steaming pile...

'—where you're going.'

...of something disgusting.

She stared down at her foot, and then back at him. 'What am I standing in?'

'Horse manure.'

He didn't offer to help. In fact he didn't do anything at all. Gritting her teeth, she lifted her foot clear of the mess and placed it on firmer ground, closing her eyes when the stuffed squished between her toes like slimy, putrid mud.

To her disbelief, when she opened them again she found the man making as if to lie back down on his trolley and disappear beneath the tractor again.

'I'll finish up here, and then I'll show you your room.'

'No!'

She didn't mean to snap, but the stuff oozing between her toes had started her stomach roiling and churning—again. If she was going to throw up—again—today, she wanted that to happen in the privacy of a bathroom, not on some roadside and certainly not in this man's barn.

Nobody had warned her that being pregnant could make her feel so awful. Surely the very definition of morning sickness was sickness that happened *in the morning*. Not all day!

She'd never stepped in horse manure before so she didn't know what her reaction in an unpregnant state might be. But in her current ten-weeks-gone condition her scalp started to tighten and a film of perspiration clung to her skin, making her oppressively clammy.

She pointed to her foot. She didn't look at it. She didn't trust her stomach to cope with the sight. 'Lead me to a tap. Now!'

She thought he was going to refuse, but with a cut-off oath he strode out of the barn's double doors back towards the house. Keira half-limped, half-squelched after him. Back in the sunlight, she dragged in deep breaths of air—cleansing breaths. The faint breeze cooled her skin, rescuing her from the worst of her clamminess.

Her scowling host slammed to a halt and pointed to a tap situated to one side of the back steps. Keira hobbled over to it, turned it on—hard—and shoved her foot, platform shoe and all, beneath the jet of water, uncaring that it soaked the bottoms of her three-quarter-length jeans. When she was sure she could bend down without falling over, she unbuckled her shoe and left it where it fell, and set to scrubbing her foot clean, ridding herself of the smell that had made her stomach rebel so violently.

When that was done she hobbled across to the back steps, sat, then shoved her head between her knees and concentrated on her breathing.

She was aware of Mr Hillier's stunned surveillance— irritation emanated from him in tidal waves of folded arms and half-muttered imprecations. Thankfully, though, he didn't address anything to her directly. Finally the nausea receded, and she was able to lift her head and meet his gaze.

And then wished she hadn't. His lip had curled. He was staring at her as if she was something unmentionable that had crawled out from beneath a rock.

'Do you threaten to faint every time you step in horse manure?'

She opened her mouth to tell him horse manure wasn't an occupational hazard in the city, but her mind got sidetracked when the actual sight of him finally registered—when her eyes flashed an unforgettable image to her brain. He stood with legs apart and hands on hips. She doubted whether he cared two hoots about how he came across physically, but whether he meant it to or not his current posture showed off the length of his legs, the strength of his thighs, not to mention the breadth of those shoulders, to perfection.

The woman in her heartily approved of all that masculine

muscle and texture. The physiotherapist, however, noted how tension gathered in the muscles of his neck and shoulders, not to mention his back. If this man wasn't careful he'd end up with a frozen shoulder or—

One of those dark eyebrows lifted. In the next instant heat flooded through her as she tore her gaze away.

She hadn't been staring! She hadn't!

Liar.

She dragged herself to her feet. 'I had a touch of car sickness,' she mumbled, as if that could explain everything. 'I, um, I have groceries in the car that I really ought to unpack.'

'Groceries?'

The snapped-out word had her swinging back to him. His gaze had narrowed. 'You do understand that all you're renting from me is a room? This isn't some fancy bed and breakfast or farm stay holiday.'

This was the country hospitality she was to expect? Keira drew herself up to her full height. 'Mr Hillier—' she injected her voice with as much ice as he '—the agency with whom you advertised your room assured me I would have the use of a kitchen to prepare my own meals.'

Since becoming pregnant she rarely ate out. And in the last couple of days it hadn't been just because she was frantically saving her pennies now she had a baby on the way, but because unfamiliar cooking smells assaulted her in a way they never had before, making her sick. It seemed safer to stay away from restaurants.

She glared. 'Are you telling me I've been given the wrong information?'

He stared at her as if appalled at the thought of sharing his kitchen with her. He made no reply. Keira had to blink and swallow and fight hard to keep her shoulders from slumping. 'I understand that it's only two weeks till Christmas, and that this is a busy time of year. I've obviously arrived at an inconvenient time for you and your family. I won't bother you any further. I'll take my obviously outdated assumptions about old-fashioned country hospitality and make other arrangements.'

She spun around and headed for her car. It was only after she turned the corner of the house that she realised she'd left her soiled shoe behind. She didn't break stride. She wasn't going back for it. It was ruined now anyway.

What the—?

She was leaving without even *looking* at the room? She'd dragged him away from his tractor, when there'd only been one more nut to tighten, for *this*?

Luke considered letting her just leave. The truth was he'd rather undergo a root canal than rent out his room to a woman like her. At least at the dentist's he wasn't expected to make polite conversation. Old-fashioned country hospitality? He didn't have time for that kind of nonsense. He had a farm to run.

He shifted his weight. The thing was she'd paid her week's rent up front. And he'd already spent it on a deposit for the hire of next month's combine harvester.

'Wait!' He swept up her shoe and set off after her. 'You've already paid for the room.' And he didn't want to dip into the overdraft to provide her with a refund.

She didn't turn around.

'And you've forgotten your shoe.'

She whirled around at that. 'It's ruined!'

'No, it's not.' Typical city girl. Get a bit of honest dirt on something and it was instantly unsalvageable. No concept of recycling or making do. But then he noticed her sandal still had greenish streaks of horse manure clinging to it. He pulled the rag from the back of his jeans and set to wiping it clean.

It took a major effort of will not to curl his lip at the sandal—two-inch cork platforms with a criss-crossing of colourful straps. This wasn't so much a shoe as a silly piece of confection. A bit like the lady herself.

He glanced at her again and his skin grew tight. She was too young, too fresh and pretty, too...shiny. It hurt his eyes to look at her.

She folded her arms and tapped a foot. 'Well, that's an improvement.'

He snapped to, glanced down, and found that while he'd been busy cataloguing every line of her face he'd streaked her shoe with grease. He cut back something rude and succinct. Black streaks slashed through the green ones, in some spots completely replacing them. There was no way he'd get that grease out.

Nice one, Hillier. How are you going to convince the lady to stay now?

'I'll pay for the damage,' he found himself offering.

'Not necessary. They only cost me five dollars in a sale and, believe me, I've had my five dollars' worth out of them. But...'

She stared at the sandal, lips pursed, and then she glanced up at him. That glance—it hit him square in the chest. Her eyes were grey—a clear, light grey that somehow picked up and reflected the colour of her surroundings. At the moment he could pick out flecks of green from the nearby bottlebrush tree, blue from the sky, and gold from the swaying fields of wheat. He blinked, floundered, and tried to find his centre of gravity.

'Have you wiped all that disgusting stuff off?'

By 'disgusting stuff' he figured she meant the horse manure. He'd never seen anyone react so irrationally to a bit of dung before.

He reminded himself about the overdraft, and the fact she was only staying for one week. If he could calm her down and convince her to stay, that was.

He made a show of checking the shoe carefully. 'There's

a stain here and here—' he showed her '—but the shoe itself
is clean.'

'So...it doesn't smell of...?'

God give him strength. 'No, it doesn't smell of...' His voice
trailed off in a mocking imitation of hers before he could help
himself.

Thankfully, she didn't seem to notice. Instead she took the
shoe and surveyed it. 'Do you think I could black the cork
somehow? I know they only cost five dollars, but they're so
comfortable.'

He tried to hide his surprise. 'You could give it a go.' He
doubted if the end result would set the world of fashion on
fire, but he was determined to humour her.

And then just like that she bent down and slid the sandal
back onto her foot as if it had never touched 'disgusting stuff.'
In the process, though, she overbalanced and had to grab his
arm for support.

It was not that he wasn't happy to lend that support—it
was better than her landing flat on her face—but she let go so
quickly, and then she blushed. Like she had at the back steps,
when she'd realised she'd been caught out staring at him. And
he wasn't happy about that—the reminder of his own reaction
to that steady appraisal and the feminine appreciation that had
momentarily lit her face. It had flooded him with hormones
he'd forgotten all about, filling him with a primitive need he'd
done his best to disown.

He took a step back, fighting the urge to rub the imprint
of her hand from his skin. She was soft and warm.

He didn't do soft and warm.

She smelt like vanilla.

Trouble. That was the word that flashed through his mind.
His every instinct told him this woman was trouble.

She wore a pair of three-quarter-length jeans and a hot
pink top that tied at the waist and left her shoulders bare.

He tried to dismiss her as pale and skinny.

It didn't work. She wasn't pale. Her skin gleamed, luminous like ivory. It wasn't the kind of skin that would tan in the sun—if it got burned it would blister and peel—but to call it pale didn't do it justice. And skinny? He swallowed. Those jeans were a snug fit. Too snug. She might be slender, but she had hips that flared, a waist that curved in, and breasts that would fit in the palms of—

He cut that thought dead.

Her gaze speared back to him. 'Give me one good reason why I should stay at Candlebark?'

He forced his mind from the shape of her lips. 'Follow me.' He led her up the front steps and around to the side of the veranda. 'Look at that.' He gestured to the view. 'It can't be beaten.' He stared at the thousands of swaying heads of wheat and some of the tension eased out of him.

She glanced at it, and then back at him. 'Well…it is kind of pretty,' she allowed.

He folded his arms. 'The perfect place for a country holiday.'

'But I'm not here on holiday.'

He unfolded his arms and tried to think of something else that might tempt her. She'd said something about country hospitality. He pointed to a nearby bench. 'That's a great spot to have coffee in the morning. And, um…' He scratched a hand through his hair. 'And for a glass of wine in the evenings.' That sounded hospitality-ish, didn't it?

Her lips twitched. 'So that's your selling point is it—an old bench?'

It wasn't that old! It… Okay, perhaps it was. But—

'And as I'm currently abstaining from both caffeine and alcohol…'

He slammed his hands to his hips. This woman had turned being difficult into an art form!

'Still, if you substitute chamomile tea for coffee…'

He gave up trying to read her expression from the corner of

his eye and turned to face her fully. She met his gaze without blinking. Her hair—red-gold—tumbled around her face and shoulders in a riot of messed up curls and wispy bits, fizzing up around her sunglasses. It made her look wild and full of mischief, like an errant fairy.

Luke swallowed. He needed water. A long, cold glass of water. He was so dry. He couldn't remember the last time thirst had plagued him with such ferocity.

He cleared his throat and stared back out at his wheat. 'Look, I'm sorry about earlier. I thought you were after some kind of hokey family-farm-stay. Candlebark isn't set up for that sort of thing. I usually only rent the room out to temporary mine workers. It's coming up to harvest, and I'm too busy to...'

He trailed off. The words that had sprung to mind were *play host*. He wasn't a host. He was a landlord, and she was a temporary—very temporary—lodger. 'And of course you have full access to the kitchen while you're here. You can use the dining and living rooms too if you want.' No skin off his nose. He didn't care if she took over the entire house. He was hardly ever in it anyhow.

She surveyed him for a minute, and then she grinned. That off-balance thing happened to him again.

'Help me unload the car?'

He shrugged. 'Yeah, sure.'

'Then I guess you have yourself a guest for the next week, Mr Hillier.'

Lodger, not guest. He bit back the correction and reminded himself about the hospitality thing. 'Luke,' he offered from between gritted teeth. 'Why don't you call me Luke?'

He followed her out to her car and tried not to notice how sweetly she filled out those jeans of hers. He'd carry her bags in and then he was getting back to his tractor. Fast.

Luke returned to the barn and the relatively uncomplicated workings of his tractor. Finishing up the repairs—the tightening of that single nut—took roughly forty-five seconds.

He stowed his tools and then glared at the pile of horse dung that had so offended his 'guest'. The look on her face when she'd stood in the stuff! He seized a spade. The last thing he needed was a repeat performance. He mucked out the horse stalls and removed all signs of horse manure from the barn and its immediate surrounds. That took half an hour.

Next he set about cleaning the tack. He rubbed leather conditioner into his saddle, all the while searching his brain for anything else she might find offensive about the farm—anything as earthy as horse manure, that was—but he came up with a blank. Since Jason's border collie had died—hit by a car eight months ago—he, Jason and the horses were the only living, breathing beings on Candlebark. As long as you didn't count snakes, spiders, lizards, the odd kangaroo or ten, possums, bees and hornets.

He let rip with an oath. What if something else spooked her? What if she just upped and left without so much as a by-your-leave after all?

He threw his cloth down. He'd planned to start clearing the western boundary paddock this afternoon. Get it ready for sowing in April. At the moment it was choked with Paterson's Curse. He sighed and admitted defeat. He wouldn't get out there today. He'd best stay close to the homestead in case anything set his 'guest' off again.

He didn't doubt his first instinct about her—that she was trouble with a capital T—but her money was as good as the next person's, and for the next three weeks—until they had the harvest in—every penny counted.

He glanced at his watch. He'd shown her to her room roughly an hour and a half ago. At least she couldn't complain about that! Her room was big and clean. Spotless, in fact. Luke knew because he scrubbed it to within an inch of its life every week.

But if ants had invaded the pantry again or if, heaven forbid, she caught sight of a mouse...

His temples started to pound and an ache stretched behind his eyes. He wanted nothing more than to get into his ute and bolt—lose himself in the wide plains and open skies of his land. He set his mouth and strode outside. With one longing glance at the swaying fields of gold, he turned towards the house.

He found his lodger in the kitchen, waiting for the jug to boil. A box—in fact several boxes—of herbal tea snuggled up against his jar of instant coffee. A loaf of bread nestled next to the already full breadbox—one of those fancy boutique loaves that were more seed than bread. He didn't know why people bothered. If they wanted seeds, why didn't they just buy seeds?

A women's magazine and a local real-estate guide graced the table. He rolled his shoulders, stretched his neck first to the left and then to the right. He was hardly ever in the house—who cared where she put her stuff?

The jug came to the boil and Keira reached for a mug—his mug. He opened his mouth. He shut it again with a snap. What did it matter what mug she used?

She gestured to the teas and coffee, sent him one of those seemingly effortless smiles of hers. 'Would you like one?'

'No, thanks.'

He didn't want her thinking long, lazy afternoon teas or leisurely meals were commonplace around here. He'd stopped work to make sure she had everything she needed, that she was reasonably comfortable. End of story.

'Is everything up to scratch?' His voice came out rusty, as if he hadn't used it in a long time. 'Are you happy with your room?'

'It's more than adequate, thank you.'

Adequate?

'I cleared a shelf in the fridge and another in the pantry for my things. I hope that's okay?'

'Perfectly.' He worked hard at keeping his tone neutral.

She was here for one week—seven days. After today they'd be lucky to spend more than five minutes in each other's company. He just wanted to make sure she hadn't gone and got spooked again.

'Oh.' She swung around from pouring boiling water into his—her—mug. 'You have ants in the pantry. Thought I'd best warn you.'

He rubbed a hand across the back of his neck and steeled himself for outrage.

'My grandmother used to leave a jar of honey open for them in our pantry. They seemed to leave everything else alone after that.'

He stopped rubbing his nape and steeling himself to stare at her. She'd turned back to jiggle her teabag. 'Let me get this straight. Ants don't faze you, but a bit of horse dung has you running for cover?'

Actually, it had frozen her to the spot and had turned her a deathly shade of green.

She stilled, but didn't turn around. She jiggled her teabag with renewed enthusiasm. 'Haven't you ever had an irrational aversion to anything before?'

You bet! Going into town, for one, and having to endure the stares, the speculation in strangers' eyes as they were no doubt trying to assess if what his in-laws said about him was true.

She dropped her teabag into the kitchen tidy, then turned with hands on hips. He answered with a non-committal shrug. Her lips twitched, as if something funny had just occurred to her. 'I bet I could name a few things you'd be averse to—male cologne, skin care products.'

He stiffened. Did he smell? 'Perfume's for girls,' he growled. So was that goop they slathered on their faces. And he didn't smell of anything worse than honest sweat! 'Right?' he demanded of Jason, who had chosen that moment to slouch into the kitchen.

'Whatever,' Jason muttered.

Luke heaved back a sigh. Some time in the last few months Jason had turned into a moody, brooding teenager, with all the communication skills of a bad-tempered bull. 'This is Ms Keely. She's staying here for the next week.'

Another grunt.

'This is my son, Jason.'

Keira beamed one of those smiles at his son, and held her hand out across the table towards him. 'It's nice to meet you, Jason. And, please, call me Keira.'

Jason stared at Keira's outstretched hand without moving. When he finally shuffled forward to shake it, Luke let out a breath he hadn't even known he'd been holding.

'Jason's fourteen.' For the life of him, Luke didn't know why he'd parted with that particular piece of information.

'Nearly fifteen!' Jason glared, and then he shuffled his feet. 'I though you were clearing the boundary paddock?'

'I'm a bit behind schedule.' Luke managed not to glance at Keira as he said it. 'Tractor had an oil leak.'

Jason stared down at his feet. 'Need a hand?'

'Nah, it's all good.' It wasn't his son's responsibility to get the farm back to full running capacity—that responsibility rested on his shoulders alone. Jason should be hanging out with his friends and having fun—doing whatever teenagers did these days.

Jason scowled. 'Yeah, well, whatever.'

Keira glanced from one to the other, a tiny crease forming between her eyes. 'I…um…brought a caramel mud cake.'

She pulled an enormous box from the fridge and set on the table. When she lifted the lid the scent of cake and sweetness filled the air.

'They didn't have anything smaller than this monstrosity, but I'm afraid I couldn't resist. There's not a chance of me getting through all this on my own, so please help yourselves. It'd be a shame to let it go to waste.'

As she was talking, she cut three generous slices from the perfect round. More of that sweetness drenched the air. Luke couldn't remember the last time the kitchen had smelled so good.

'Sweet!' Jason accepted one of the slices before slouching back off in the direction of his room.

Keira glanced up at Luke, a hint of mockery lighting her eyes. 'Relax, it's only a piece of cake, Luke.' With that she gathered up her magazines, her tea, and her slice of cake. 'I'm sure you'll excuse me if I retire to your veranda to admire that view of yours.'

She left—just like that. As if she didn't need looking after, as if she didn't need that country hospitality she'd been so hot about. And without inviting him to join her.

Not that he'd wanted an invitation.

Luke stared around his now strangely colourless kitchen, his gaze coming to rest on the remaining slice of cake. From somewhere deep inside yearning gripped him. For a moment he was tempted to swipe a finger through the rich chocolate frosting.

He reached out.

What the hell...? He snapped back. Then he seized the plate and shoved it into the fridge.

He stormed out through the back door. He had work to do.

CHAPTER TWO

LUKE shot upright—still groggy from sleep—and groped for his bedside clock. Through slitted eyes he read 3:21. With a groan, he dropped it back. Something had woken him from a dead sleep. What?

Closing his eyes, he concentrated on picking out any noise unfamiliar amid the normal night sounds of crickets, cicadas, and a call from the occasional tawny frogmouth.

He relaxed when the low whine of the tap in the bathroom broke through the other night noises. His lodger. It would take him a night or two to get used to someone else's rhythms. *Good, go back to sleep.* He punched his pillow, settled back down, and…

Hold on. He lifted his head again. Sat up. That was no normal nightly visit to the bathroom. Keira was… Was she being sick?

For all of two-tenths of a second he considered burying his head in one pillow, covering it with another, and trying to go back to sleep. But he knew it wouldn't work. He'd never been able to ignore an animal in physical distress. Unfortunately, that included lodgers.

Muttering imprecations under his breath, he hauled himself out of bed, dragged on a pair of tracksuit pants to cover his nakedness and made for the bathroom. *Trouble with a capital T!*

He paused outside the door, hand raised to knock, and

then grimaced at the unmistakable sounds that emerged from behind the door—muffled but unmistakable. 'Keira?' He knocked. 'Can I come in?' He wanted to burst in and make sure she was all right, so he could go back to bed. He held himself back, reminding himself she was a lone woman in a strange place.

Behind the door came movement... The door opened, and all his irritation fled. He'd thought she'd looked pale when he'd first clapped eyes on her, but now she was white. The only colour in her face came from the grey of her eyes, but even they were dim and bloodshot. All that red-gold hair fizzing around her face only made her look paler.

His heart lurched. 'Is there anything I can get for you? Would you like me to take you to the hospital or—?'

She shook her head. 'I'm really sorry I disturbed you, Luke. I—'

She turned from white to green. She spun away to kneel in front of the toilet and was immediately and comprehensively sick. Again. Luke leapt forward to drag her hair back from her face. He didn't try to talk, and he didn't rub her back because he didn't know if that would make her feel better or worse, but with every heaving retch his heart clenched harder and tighter.

When this particular bout of sickness had passed, he flushed the toilet, closed its lid and settled her on top of it. When he was certain she wasn't going to fall, he moistened a facecloth and very gently wiped her face.

She didn't open her eyes until he was finished. 'You're very kind,' she whispered.

No, he wasn't. But he couldn't stand by and do nothing if she was sick. 'What did you eat today?'

She frowned. It turned into a glare. 'I can tell you one thing—I am *never* eating caramel mud cake again. I couldn't resist another piece after dinner, but... Ugh, never again.'

It almost made him smile. Only he couldn't smile when

she remained so pale. 'Keira, I really think you should see a doctor.'

She pulled in a breath. 'It's nothing. I promise.' She closed her eyes and pulled in another breath. 'It's become the norm over the last few days, that's all.' A third breath. 'I'm sure it'll pass.'

His head snapped back. The norm? She was slender, sure, but he hadn't pegged her as anorexic or bulimic. Still, she was young and pretty, and he knew women her age felt an enormous pressure to conform to impossible media images. Not for the first time he was grateful he had a son instead of a daughter. Raising a daughter without the help of her mother could prove tricky. Or at least trickier than a son.

Keira's confession settled it—she was seeing a doctor. Whether she had food poisoning or was bulimic or had some ghastly twenty-four hour virus, he was taking her to the hospital. Illness like this should *never* be the norm.

'C'mon.' He urged her to her feet and handed her a glass of water to rinse out her mouth. 'It's better to be safe than sorry. It'll take us no time at all to drive to the hospital and have someone check you over.' When he saw she was about to refuse he added, 'Look, I'm going to be out in the fields from dawn, and I probably won't return till late. Jason will most likely be out with his mates for most of the day. I can't guarantee there'll be anyone here to help you if you need it tomorrow.'

She smiled. She was pale and woebegone, and yet she managed a smile. He didn't know why, but it made his heart crash about in his chest. 'It's sweet of you to consider my welfare.'

Not sweet. He refused to allow that. He just didn't want another woman's death on his conscience.

'Luke, I'm really not sick.'

He raised an eyebrow at that.

'And I have seen a doctor.'

His shoulders loosened a fraction. The pressure eased from his chest. In the next moment the pressure crashed back. If she was this sick after seeing a doctor then that indicated something serious—something sinister.

'I have nothing worse,' she continued, 'than a bad bout of morning sickness.'

He stared at her, trying to make sense of her words. Morning sickness? But that meant...

'I'm pregnant.'

And then she beamed. His legs gave out, plonking him down to sit on the side of the bathtub.

She sat down again too. 'I'm having a baby.'

Only then did he notice that she wore an oversized sleep-shirt in powder blue. It had a picture of a teddy bear on the front and hung down to her knees. She didn't look old enough to have a baby!

He surged to his feet as an unlooked-for and unwanted wave of protectiveness flooded him. 'Where's your baby's father? Why the hell is he letting you go through this on your own?'

'Oh, Luke...'

She pressed two fingers to her mouth. Luke immediately went on high alert. 'Are you going to be sick again?' He readied himself to hold her hair back from her face if the need arose. He glanced at that hair. For all its curly unruliness, it had felt smooth and soft in his hand.

'No, I don't think so. I think I might risk a cup of tea.'

Her colour had started to return. He shuffled back a step. *Pregnant!* 'Do you need a hand with anything else?'

'No, I'm fine now. Honest.'

With a nod he backed out through the door. 'Right. I'll go put the jug on.'

'Oh, that's not necessary. You can go back to bed and I...'

He didn't turn or stop. He headed straight for the kitchen.

Pregnant and alone in the world—he'd read that fact in her eyes.

Trouble with a capital T!

He couldn't get involved. He couldn't risk it. But the least he could do was make her a cup of tea.

When Keira entered the kitchen she was glad to find Luke had dragged a T-shirt over his bare chest. The breadth of his shoulders, those bulging biceps, had all started to filter into her consciousness towards the end there in the bathroom. It had taken a concerted effort to try and ignore the effect they were having on her.

While it had been beyond kind of him to hold back her hair, to mop her face, it had all started to feel a bit too... intimate. And she wasn't doing intimate. Not until she and the Munchkin were well and truly settled, thank you very much.

Still, there was no denying she'd gained a measure of comfort from Luke's presence, and she hadn't expected that. It had brought those niggling doubts back to the surface, though. Taking great bites out of her confidence, making her question the validity of having a baby on her own.

No!

She pushed the very idea of that thought away. She could and she *would* have this baby on her own. Those doubts—it was just the misery of nausea talking.

She saw Luke turn from surveying her various boxes of tea. Besides peppermint and chamomile, she had a selection of herbal teas made up by the boutique tea shop she walked past every day on her way to work at the hospital. The teas had gorgeous names like Enliven, Autumn Harvest and Tranquillity.

'Where's your...?' He paused, his eyes zeroing in on the way her hands fumbled with the sash of her terry towelling robe.

'Where's my what?' She gave up trying to tie a bow and

settled for a granny knot. It occurred to her that Luke might be as pleased as she that they'd both covered up a bit more. The thought made her stumble.

Stop it! It was somewhere between three and four in the morning. Nobody had rational thoughts at this time of the day. She flipped her hair out from the collar of her robe and raked her hands through it...and remembered the way he'd held it back from her face. She'd felt too sick to be embarrassed then. Strangely, she didn't feel embarrassed now either.

Luke continued to stare at her, his eyes dark and intense, and filled with a primitive hunger. It raised all the hair on her arms. Not in a panicked I'm-alone-in-a-strange-place-with-a-man-I-hardly-know kind of way either. Which would be rational. But then she'd already determined this wasn't a rational time of day.

And it was quickly in danger of becoming less so, because as she stared back at him warmth stole through all her limbs, while languor threatened to rob her of her strength...and of the last shreds of her sanity.

One of them had to be rational. Think of the Munchkin!

'You want to know something amazing?' She didn't wait for his answer. 'All my baby's fingers can be separately identified now, and soon its eyes will be fully formed.'

He jerked, and muttered something she pretended not to hear.

Talking about her baby didn't douse her in cold, rational logic, but at least it had Luke swinging away. She wanted to shake herself, shake the warmth from her limbs, but she didn't trust that her stomach would tolerate that kind of punishment just yet.

She frowned and remembered to ask again, 'Where's my what?'

'Liquorice tea.'

She collapsed at the kitchen table and massaged her temples. Of all the things he might have asked her... 'Why would

I have liquorice tea?' She'd never heard of the stuff before. And, quite frankly, it didn't sound all that inviting.

'It's a morning sickness cure.'

She lifted her head. 'Really?'

'So's eating liquorice.'

She watched, half in disbelief, as he sliced a lemon, dropped the slice into a mug, and then poured boiling water over it. He set the mug in front of her. 'Sip that. It should help settle your stomach.'

He made himself some tea and sat opposite. Keira pulled the pad and pen resting on the table towards her and wrote down 'liquorice, liquorice tea, lemon'—before taking an experimental sip from her mug. 'I'm ten weeks pregnant, but the morning sickness has only hit me in the last few days. I haven't had a chance to research cures yet.'

He shrugged. 'Ginger can be good. Ginger biscuits, dry ginger ale—that sort of thing.'

He blew on his tea before taking a sip, and it was only then, through the mirage of steam, that she realised his eyes weren't black, as she'd originally thought, but a deep, rich brown.

When he kinked a questioning eyebrow, she dragged her gaze away and added 'ginger' to her list. 'I'll pop into town tomorrow.'

'Has it been happening mostly at night?'

'It's been happening all over the place.' Why hadn't anyone warned her about this?

'Having something in your stomach is supposed to help. When you go to bed take a banana or some biscuits with you. When you wake up through the night just have a bite or two. It'll help.'

'How on earth do you know all this?' She took another sip of her lemon and hot water concoction. Her stomach was starting to calm down. 'Don't get me wrong. I'm grateful. I really think this is working.'

He set his mug down with a snap. 'Tammy, my wife, had morning sickness pretty bad with Jason.'

Of course! She glanced around. 'Is she away at the moment?' It would be nice to have another woman to talk to about all this.

'She's dead.'

Keira froze, and then very slowly turned back. She knew exactly how wide her eyes had gone, but for the life of her she couldn't make them go back to their normal size.

'She died three years ago.' The words dropped out of him, curt and emotionless.

Oh! 'Oh, Luke, I'm so sorry.' Idiot! Anyone with eyes in their head could see this place lacked a woman's touch. Perhaps that explained why there were no Christmas decorations, too.

'It was three years ago,' he repeated, his voice flat.

As if three years meant anything!

He might not look heartbroken—she suspected Luke Hillier was not the kind of man to wear his heart on his sleeve—but it explained why he looked so worn out, run down...worn down. She promptly forgave him for all his gruffness and shortness to her earlier in the day.

'I don't think it matters if it's been three years, five years or ten years. My mother died ten years ago and I still miss her.' Especially at this time of year.

'Tammy and I had already separated before she died. A separation I instigated.'

Her heart lurched at the pain that momentarily twisted his features. What? Did he think that meant he wasn't deserving of sympathy? 'You and Tammy had a child together. That's a bond that can never be broken.' And Jason—how he must ache for Jason's loss.

'Says you...' his lips twisted '...who's having a baby on her own.'

Yes, well, there was a good reason for that. But he didn't

give her a chance to explain. He shot to his feet and tipped what was left of his tea down the sink. 'I'm going back to bed.'

He almost made it to the door before spinning back to the pantry. He grabbed a packet of digestives and shoved them at her. 'Take these to bed with you, just in case.'

She stared at them and willed her heart to stop its unaccountable softening.

'Thank you. For everything,' she added, but doubted he heard. He'd already disappeared.

Keira pulled up short the next morning when she found Luke seated at the kitchen table, reading the Sunday paper. She'd expected him to be long gone out into those fields of his. It was one of the reasons she'd allowed herself the luxury of a lie-in—knowing she wouldn't be disturbing anyone. Given the kind of night she'd had, it had seemed a perfectly reasonable proposition. But if Luke had delayed his work to make sure she was okay...

'Good morning.' She tried to keep her voice casual, not sure exactly what tone she should be aiming for after last night.

Luke immediately set the paper aside, leapt to his feet and slotted two slices of her nine-grain bread into the toaster before turning back, hands on hips, to examine her. 'Well?' he demanded. 'How are you feeling?'

She couldn't resist teasing him. 'If I'm going to get waited on like this, then I'm at death's door.'

He frowned.

'Relax, Luke. I'm fine. I slept like a log when I went back to bed—' which wasn't exactly the truth '—and I wasn't sick again.'

That, though, was. Thankfully. And she didn't want him feeling responsible for her. She was more than capable of looking after herself and the Munchkin, thank you.

She *really* didn't want her heart lurching at the mere sight of the man either. There was no future in that.

She sat. 'I mean it, Luke. You need to relax,' she repeated when he retrieved her toast and set it in front of her. He returned from the pantry with his arms laden with spreads.

She opened her mouth to protest some more, but suddenly she was ravenously hungry and allowed herself to be side-tracked long enough to slather butter and strawberry jam over one slice of toast. 'Oh, this is divine,' she groaned, devouring it and repeating the process with the second slice. When she was finished she leant back in her chair with a sigh. 'How on earth is it possible to feel so sick just a few short hours ago and now be so hungry?'

'It's normal.'

That was when she remembered what she had to tell him. She had to set him straight. 'Luke, I'm not some pathetic piece who's accidentally found herself pregnant and then been dumped by some low-down, lying snake in the grass.' She could see that was what he thought.

'It's none of my business.' He shot to his feet. 'Would you like more toast?'

No, she didn't want more toast. She didn't want him making her feel all warm and fuzzy inside either.

'For the last twelve months I've been on an IVF programme.' She waited to see if her words made any impression on him.

He bent down to survey the contents of the fridge. 'What about a piece of fruit or a yoghurt?'

'Did you hear what I just said? I've fallen pregnant deliberately. *And* I've chosen to do it on my own.'

He stopped fussing at the fridge to turn and stare. 'What on earth would you go and do something like that for?'

Now that she had his attention—and, oh my, she certainly had that—she wasn't sure she wanted it. 'You...um...

might like to close the fridge door. It's shaping up to be a warm day.'

'You… But… You're too young!'

She blinked. And then she grinned. 'How old do you think I am? I'm twenty-four—old enough to know my own mind.'

Luke sat, scratched both hands back through his hair while he stared at her. 'But you're still so young. You're attractive…'

Her heart did that stupid leaping around thing again.

'Do you have something against men?'

'No!' She stared at him in horror, but she could suddenly see how he'd come to that conclusion. 'I had an infected ovary removed when I was nineteen. In the last couple of years my remaining ovary has started to develop cysts, and it looks like it will have to go as well. And soon.'

'So medically…?'

'If I want a baby, I have to look at doing it now.'

He sat back, let out a low whistle.

'I mean, in an ideal world I'd have found the man of my dreams and we'd…' She trailed off. She wasn't anti-men, not by any stretch, but she wasn't sure she believed in the man of her dreams either.

'That's a heck of a decision to be faced with—and to do it on your own.' Luke leaned towards her, his hand clenched and his eyebrows drawing down low over his eyes. 'Being a single parent—you have no idea how hard it is. You could've found a man who'd have been happy to help you out.' He shook his head. 'It would've spared you the expense of IVF, and going through your pregnancy alone.'

'And given me a whole new set of problems,' she pointed out. But her heart burned for him. He and his wife might have already been separated, but her death had obviously wounded him. He'd certainly never expected to become a single father. That much was evident.

She'd known Luke Hillier for less than twenty-four hours,

but last night he'd held her hair back from her face while she'd vomited. She figured that gave her a certain insight into the man. She leant across the table towards him. She wanted to reach across and touch his hand—perhaps because his eyes were so dark and his mouth so grim? Perhaps because she sensed that behind the grimness lay genuine concern? 'Would you ever marry a woman just because you wanted a baby?'

'No!'

Tension shot through his shoulders. The physiotherapist in her itched to un-knot all that tightness. The thought made the woman in her turn to putty.

Oh, *puhlease*—pregnancy hormones were addling her brain!

'I...' She swallowed, edged back in her seat. 'I couldn't use someone like that either. In the end I had to make a decision I could live with.'

He gazed at her for a long moment and finally gave a curt nod. She could have sworn she saw admiration flash in those dark eyes of his, and it warmed her all the way down to her toes. She couldn't help smiling at him, and just like that an arc of electricity vibrated between them. Keira's heart, pulse, spirits—all started to race.

She dragged her gaze away and forced herself to stare at the strawberry jam. This...this heat that seemed to spring up between them—she had to ignore it. In one week she'd be leaving here, and she and Luke would never clap eyes on each other again. She was here to secure her and the Munchkin's future. She had no intention of getting sidetracked by a sculpted chest and a pair of dark, smouldering eyes. She had no intention of getting used to someone looking out for her. She was an independent woman of the new millennium. She didn't need any of that nonsense.

She lifted her chin. 'I know common wisdom has it that raising a child on one's own is harder, but I'm not a hundred percent convinced of that.'

He raised an eyebrow. How on earth one eyebrow could contain such a depth of scepticism she would never know. Doubts crowded around her, but she pushed them back. She came from a long line of strong women. She was more than capable of providing a good home and a good life for her baby.

'Tell me that after months of broken sleep, colic, and a bad case of the baby blues,' he drawled.

'My father deserted my mother when she was pregnant with me. She raised me on her own. I don't doubt things were hard for her at times, but she was strong and resourceful and full of life.' Keira refused to let her chin drop. She would not let the picture his words had created spook her. 'I had a wonderful childhood, and I certainly never felt anything was lacking from my life.' And her Munchkin wouldn't either!

'I didn't mean—'

'In fact—' she spoke over the top of him '—I'd say my childhood was better than a lot of my friends who had both parents.' Especially if those parents were either divorced or constantly arguing.

Her two best friends had been cases in point, their loyalties torn between their parents. Keira had always considered herself lucky in comparison. She and her mother—they'd been incredibly close. When her mother had died, her grandmother—another strong female role model—had stepped into the breach, helping Keira through the worst of her grief. Keira was determined to follow in their footsteps, to uphold their examples.

Her mother had always claimed it was foolhardy for a woman to pin all her hopes on a man, that first and foremost a woman should rely on herself. Keira believed that with all her heart. She knew her mother would have applauded her decision to pursue IVF and have a baby on her own. The knowledge that she'd have made her mother proud kept her going when doubts plagued her.

And she wasn't going to let some man who seemed to spend less than ten minutes a day in his own son's company make her doubt herself either!

Tell me that after months of broken sleep.

Her mouth went dry. 'I will love my baby, and I don't need virtual strangers telling me I'm not up to the task!'

She loved her baby already. Her hand curved around her stomach. It wouldn't be flat for too much longer. Soon there would be ample evidence of the baby growing inside her, and she couldn't wait. 'I want this baby with every fibre of my being.' She couldn't wait to hold it in her arms, to count all its fingers and toes, to touch the down on its head. 'That's what will get me through the colic and the sleepless nights and the hormone swings and…and everything!'

She glared at Luke, but couldn't prevent her heart from sinking just a tiny bit when she watched the bond that had started to form between them dissolve utterly.

He stood, his face shuttered and his eyes more black than brown. 'Looks like you have everything under control, then.'

She folded her arms. 'I do.'

She did!

'Good. I don't have time to…waste.' He seized his hat and jammed it on his head. 'There's work to be done.' With that, he strode out through the back door.

Keira stared after him. 'Well, why didn't you just say you don't have time to mollycoddle pregnant women?' she muttered. It was obvious that was what he'd meant. Well, she didn't need mollycoddling. She hadn't asked him to mollycoddle.

Still, she couldn't help feeling she'd just thrown his kindness back in his face with a considerable lack of grace. And now she had a whole day to kill, with nothing to do.

She cleared away the breakfast things and then spied the shopping list she'd made earlier. Much earlier. Right. She shoved it in her pocket. The supermarket in Gunnedah would be open, and she'd do just about anything to avoid a repeat of last night's bout of illness—even if that meant drinking something as odd as liquorice tea.

Keira's natural buoyancy reasserted itself as she negotiated her way down Gunnedah's main street. How could it not? The town overflowed with a festive spirit that was nowhere to be seen at Candlebark.

Christmas carols spilled out from the shops and onto the street. Fake snow and tinsel festooned every shop window. Santa displays abounded—Santa in a sleigh, Santa in his workshop with his elves—so did angels and stars. She stopped by a shop window containing a nativity scene, stared at the baby Jesus in the manger. Her hand crept across her stomach. 'Oh, Munchkin, you just wait till next Christmas. We're going to have so much fun!'

This time of year always reminded Keira of her mother. Carmel Keely had adored Christmas—adorning every room of their apartment with Christmas decorations, baking for weeks beforehand, always grumbling that their ginormous tree was far too big for their apartment, which it was, but never replacing it. And every year she, her mother and her grandmother had sat down to a full Christmas dinner with all the trimmings. It had always been a special day. Her mother had made sure of that. And this year Keira knew she'd miss her mother and her grandmother just that little bit more than normal.

She wondered what Luke and Jason did for Christmas. Then frowned. It was kind of hard, imagining Luke being festive.

She chewed her bottom lip, drawing to a halt as she recalled the expression on his face when he'd told her that his wife was dead. Her heart burned. Poor Jason. She knew from experience how hard this time of year could be. Luke had to try and make Christmas special for his son all on his own now.

Just like you'll be doing.

Yeah, but she'd chosen that path. Luke hadn't.

With a heart that had started to feel heavier with every passing second, she recalled how she'd all but told Luke to butt out and keep his opinions to himself this morning. After he'd held her hair back and had mopped her face…and made her lemon and hot water…and given her morning sickness remedies. He was obviously busy with the farm, but he'd taken a significant portion of the morning off to make sure she was okay…*and to make her breakfast*!

She was a shrew. It wasn't his fault her insecurities had momentarily got the better of her.

She bit her lip and glanced around, as if this country street could provide her with inspiration for how to make amends.

Her eyes lit on the Chinese restaurant across the road. She sucked her bottom lip all the way into her mouth. She could cook dinner tonight, couldn't she? That would at least save Luke some of that precious time of his.

Her spirits started to lift again. Maybe this evening Luke and Jason could eat together. Last night they'd simply seized their plates and shot off to separate parts of the house—Luke to what she guessed was his study, and Jason to watch television in the living room. She'd watched in stunned amazement and sworn that she and her child would never end up like that. But if Luke had more time…

The chicken and hokkien noodle stir-fry she'd prepared was ready to serve at precisely the same moment Luke walked through the back door. Keira took it as a good sign—all the planets magically aligned, or something.

'Hi.' She turned from the stove with a grin she hoped hid the nerves that unaccountably assailed her.

She had absolutely nothing to be nervous about. This dinner—it was nothing more than a friendly gesture.

Luke stared at the table set for three, and then at the food simmering on the stove. There was a lot of it. She'd figured a man of the land and a growing teenage boy would have hearty appetites.

He raised an eyebrow. Keira suddenly hated that eyebrow with a vengeance.

'Expecting company?' he drawled.

'Of course not.' But it was hard to get the words out because her throat had started to close over. 'I… This…' She swallowed. Did he hate chicken, or had he taken an unaccountable dislike to her since this morning?

She cleared her throat and gestured across the hallway to the living room, where Jason lay sprawled on the sofa with the television blaring. 'I thought I'd cook dinner for everyone tonight.'

She couldn't stand the way he was looking at her, so she grabbed a plate and turned away to start dishing out food. Luke moved to stand behind her. Close. Keira stilled, her hand trembling as his heat beat at her. She hadn't even heard him move.

'I don't want you doing this ever again.' His voice was low, but its fury sliced through her. 'You hear me?'

She swallowed and nodded.

'Jason and I don't need your charity, and we sure as hell don't need your pity. You can go practise your home-making skills somewhere else. Got it?'

The unfairness of his accusations had her spine stiffening. 'Loud and clear,' she snapped, shoving the laden plate at him. 'Believe me, I won't make the same mistake again.' She pushed the serving spoon under his nose. 'But while we're on the subject of home-making, from what I can see I'm not the one who needs to brush up on that particular skill set.'

His mouth opened and closed but no sound came out.

'And, for your information, cooking dinner was my oh-so-stupid attempt to try and make up for throwing your routine out this morning. *Nothing* more.'

And then she lifted her voice, so it could be heard over the television in the next room. 'There's food here if you want it, Jason.'

With a cut-off oath, Luke spun and stalked from the room. Jason slouched in. He stared after his father. 'What's up with him?'

She shrugged. 'Beats me.'

'Yeah, well, I wouldn't worry about it,' he mumbled. 'He's an old grump.'

He could say *that* again!

Jason took his laden plate back into the living room. Keira collapsed at the table, her heart thumping.

Right—from now on her and Luke's paths were on completely separate planes, trajectories whatever you wanted to call it. She'd make sure of it.

CHAPTER THREE

LUKE halted in the doorway to the living room, brought up short by the sight of Keira rifling through the sideboard. He automatically opened his mouth to ask her what the hell she was doing, but closed it again.

He had no intention of jumping to conclusions again, like he had last night.

This woman—with all her colour and her big, bright smiles—had waltzed into his neatly structured world and he'd been off balance ever since. He ground his teeth together. He was going to find that balance again if it killed him.

Last night he'd hurled words at her in an effort to stop the image of her, the very idea of what she'd represented, from tearing him apart. She'd stood there in his kitchen as if she'd had every right in the world, mocking him with her very... *perfection*!

Once upon a time he'd dreamed of that kind of life. But it could never be his. Ever.

Last night anger and grief had clawed up through him in an explosion of anguish. He'd lashed out at her before he could help himself. He wasn't losing control like that again. He might not want her rifling through his personal things, but flying off the handle wouldn't help him restore that much-needed equilibrium.

With that in mind, he straightened, shoved his hands into

the pockets of his jeans, and drawled as casually as he could, 'Can I help you?'

She half turned. 'I didn't hear you come in. I thought you'd be out in the fields all day.'

He'd come back to grab some lunch. Not that he needed to explain himself to her. 'What are you looking for?'

'The telephone directory.' She stood, hands on hips, and stared at him expectantly.

She wore white linen trousers and a lime-green shirt. She reminded him of the rainbow lorikeets that dipped through the yard in the early morning to feed in the bottlebrush trees.

'Please tell me you have at least some kind of local business directory!'

Her clothes looked summery and cool, but her cheeks were pink and her hair almost crackled. He pointed to the sideboard. 'Middle drawer.'

She spun back, located said directory, and promptly hugged it to her chest. Which made him notice exactly what a nice chest she had.

He forced his gaze to the floor, but he needn't have bothered. Keira hadn't noticed. She raced passed him to settle herself at the kitchen table. She began rifling through the directory, completely oblivious to him.

He watched her, eyes narrowed. Something was up. It was evident in the way she flicked over the pages, the way she sucked her bottom lip into her mouth.

Walk away. The lady had made it clear at breakfast yesterday that she knew what she was doing.

If he wanted lunch he couldn't walk away. It didn't mean he had to engage her in conversation, though.

He filled the jug. He pulled a loaf of bread towards him. Not speaking suddenly seemed a bit childish. He slathered butter on his bread, located the cheese and started to slice it. 'What are you looking for?' He told himself it was a perfectly harmless question.

'A local builder. A *reputable* one.'

She didn't even glance up as she spoke. Luke abandoned the cheese. 'Why?' She was only here for a week. What on earth did she need with a builder?

'Because a disreputable one won't be of any use at all.'

When she met his gaze he could see that lines of strain fanned out from her eyes. And she'd gone pale. He planted his feet. 'Have you eaten today? You can't—'

He broke off, mentally kicking himself.

She sat back and folded her arms. She didn't say anything. Not one word.

Luke stood it for as long as he could. Then he caved. 'Look, okay... Last night I was...'

'Rude?' she supplied. 'Churlish?'

'Out of order,' he ground out.

He cast another glance at her. She really was turning very pale. His hands clenched. She was having a baby. *On her own.* She didn't deserve attitude from him. 'Rude and churlish,' he admitted.

He pulled out a chair. He'd meant to plant himself in it, apologise like a man, but his spine bowed under the sudden weight that crashed down on him and he found himself slumping instead. 'This kitchen hasn't had a woman in it for a long time. Coming in last night and seeing you so at home, with dinner on and the table set...' He dragged a hand down his face. 'It...' He didn't know how to go on.

'Oh!' The word left her in one soft exhalation. 'Oh, I didn't think of that. I'm sorry, Luke. I didn't mean to rake up ghosts from the past.'

The problem was his past had never been like that—it had never been that inviting, that tempting. Fate was laughing at him, deriding him—showing him with one hand all he could have had, and then taking it away with the other.

Which was as it should be.

'I lost the plot for a moment. I'm sorry.'

Keira reached out and placed her hand over his. 'Why don't we just forget all about last night?'

He eased out a breath. The scent of vanilla rose up all around him. 'I'd like that.' He studied her face. Her colour still hadn't returned. He'd gestured towards his abandoned sandwich. 'Have you eaten?'

For some reason that made her laugh. With a self-conscious glance at her hand on his, she drew back and nodded. 'I ate earlier, thank you.'

Good. He couldn't help noticing how she flicked a glance across to the cheese, though. He reached across and relocated the breadboard from the bench to the table. He cut more cheese—far more than he'd need—and made a show of making sandwiches. 'Want one?'

'No, thank you.' But she flicked another glance at the cheese.

He pushed the breadboard towards her and bit into his sandwich. 'I always cut too much, and then it goes to waste.'

'Waste?'

He nodded. Then nearly grinned when she reached out and seized a slice and popped it into her mouth. She closed her eyes in what looked like ecstasy. Luke stopped chewing to stare. She opened her eyes, registered the expression on his face, and pale cheeks suddenly became pink.

Luke forced himself to start chewing again. He swallowed. 'You want to tell me what you want with a builder?'

She snaffled another piece of cheese. 'I...' Her lips trembled upwards in a smile that made something in his chest tighten. 'I've inherited a house in the town.'

He lowered his sandwich.

She nodded. 'I know—amazing, huh? My Great-Aunt Ada—whom I'd never met, mind—left me her house in her will.' She popped the second piece of cheese into her mouth. 'Yum!' She pointed. 'This is really good!'

'Just regular cheddar.'

She grabbed another piece. 'Apparently my great-aunt had no other living relatives. She died back in September, but it took her solicitor a couple of months to track me down.'

That smile of hers slipped and his heart dipped right along with it.

'I wish she'd tried to contact me.' She stared down at the table, one finger tracing the grain of the wood. '*I* should've contacted *her*.'

'Why?' If the woman had never been a part of her life...

'I was her last living relative. She must've been lonely towards the end.' She lifted one slim shoulder. 'And...well...she was *my* last living relative too. I'd have liked to have known her.'

Luke tried to hide his dawning horror. Not only didn't she have a partner—the father of her baby—to help her out, but she didn't have any other family either. She'd told him her mother was dead and that her father wasn't around, but what about siblings, aunts and uncles...grandparents?

For a moment she looked so forlorn and alone he found himself reaching out to squeeze her hand. To choose to have a baby with virtually no support at all—the very idea stole his breath. This woman—she had courage and strength in spades. His admiration for her grew. Right alongside that pesky protectiveness.

It wasn't his place to be protective. He didn't want to get involved. He didn't want his hormones hitting overdrive every time the scent of vanilla drifted across to him. He didn't want concerns about whether her morning sickness had returned, or if she was eating enough, if she was getting enough rest, plaguing him. His every instinct screamed *Run!*

This woman's life was none of his business.

But she had no one, and she was only here for one measly week—five more days. Helping out where he could wouldn't kill him.

'Keira, soon you'll have your baby. You'll be starting a brand new family.'

She squeezed his hand back, and that spark jumped between them again. He knew she felt it too, from the way she let go of his hand at the same moment he let go of hers, and by the way her glance skittered away.

She covered her stomach with her hand and stared down at it. He found it hard to imagine her rounded and full with child. She'd still be beautiful.

'I can hardly wait,' she said, her eyes shining.

For the first time in a long time Luke's lips stretched into a smile. It didn't hurt, it wasn't forced—merely an uncomplicated sign of pleasure at her simple sincerity and excitement. 'I forgot to say something the other night.'

Her eyes widened. 'What's that?'

A hint of breathlessness rippled through her voice. It made the surface of his skin tingle. 'I didn't congratulate you on your pregnancy. Congratulations, Keira. I wish you and your baby all the very best.'

To his astonishment, he found he wasn't merely going through the motions—he meant it. She looked as if she might actually melt, so he sat back and made his voice deliberately businesslike. 'So you've inherited this house...?'

'Which really couldn't have come at a better time. The money from the sale means I'll be able set up my own clinic in the city. I'd really love to have all that finalised before my Munchkin makes its appearance.'

'Clinic?' He shouldn't be asking about this clinic of hers. He should be asking about her aunt's house. If she needed a builder, then obviously the house needed repairs. 'What kind of clinic?'

'I'm a physiotherapist. I specialise in post-surgical rehabilitation and sports injuries. At the moment I'm working at a private hospital, but I've always dreamed of opening my own clinic.' She grinned and polished off the last of the cheese. 'And because of my great-aunt now I can.'

'You're a physio?' His jaw dropped. This slip of a girl was a physiotherapist? He didn't know why he found that so hard to believe. If he'd stopped to consider it at all, he'd have pegged her as a preschool teacher or an artist. A job where her bubbliness and enthusiasm could really shine. But a physiotherapist? It sounded so responsible and serious.

She'd look cute in a white coat, though.

Settle!

'What?' she teased. 'You don't think I'm old enough to be a physio?'

If he said yes, would that offend or flatter her? He didn't want to do either.

She threw her head back and laughed, so he settled for saying nothing. But his lips started to lift again.

'How old are *you*?'

It was a friendly challenge. He shrugged. 'Thirty-three.'

He watched her mind whirl and click, and then her eyes went wide. 'But that means you were only...' more whirring and calculating '...nineteen when Jason was born?'

'Yep.'

'And here I am, wondering if I'm truly ready for all the responsibility at twenty-four. Wow! Nineteen? That must've been hard.'

His gut clenched. 'Yep.'

When he didn't add anything else, she said, 'I'm a good physio, and I can see exactly how much tension you hold in your shoulders. If you're not careful you'll do yourself an injury. And you hold it here too.'

She lifted a hand as if to touch it to the side of his jaw. His pulse jumped. She jerked her hand back.

'Sit back in your chair like this. Nice and comfortable.'

He did as she ordered. He figured it would be easier than arguing with her.

'Now, relax the back of your tongue.'

He frowned. How on earth...?

'It's located about here.' She turned her head to the side and indicated the place. 'Concentrate hard on loosening it.'

He did. It took a moment to work out precisely what she meant, but when he finally got the hang of it a deep ripple of relaxation coursed through him. He blinked, stunned at the effect.

'You should try and remember to do that a couple of times a day.'

He nodded, but it all suddenly seemed a little too chummy—too...familiar. He didn't need anyone looking out for him. She was the one who needed help.

'Back to this house of yours.' His voice had gone gruff again, but he couldn't help it. 'I take it repairs are needed before you can sell it?'

'Apparently.'

She pulled a sheet of paper from her pocket, unfolded it, and handed it to him. It was a builder's quote—and the work it itemised was extensive. He grimaced when he read the total. 'This is going to set you back a pretty penny.' Did she have the money? Perhaps she should be looking for a banker instead?

'The real estate agency organised that last week.' She paused. 'Do you think I'm being overcharged?'

'I'm not an expert, but...' He raked his gaze down the list again. 'There's nothing that jumps out at me from this. Why?'

'Well, maybe it's just pregnancy hormones...'

'But?'

'Something seems a bit...fishy.'

'How?'

'Little things that don't seem like much but when they're added together... For example, the estate agent was supposed to take me through the house on Saturday, but something came up and he was out of the office all day… For some unspecified reason no one else could take me through in his stead.'

'Weekends *are* their busiest times.'

'I know, but when the agent took me through the house today he rushed me through it, barely giving me a chance to get a good look at anything.'

He frowned. 'Which agency?'

'The same one your room is listed with. They booked the room for me.'

'And why would they send you nearly twenty minutes out of town if all your business is *in* town?'

'Exactly. Now, admittedly I was feeling a bit queasy when I was viewing the house, so I didn't put up much of a fight, but… Have you heard any complaints about the agency?'

No—but that didn't mean anything. The few occasions when he couldn't avoid going into town he didn't speak to anyone. And no one spoke to him. He'd chosen that particular agency because, unlike the others in town, he didn't know anyone who worked there—no one who knew his parents, no one he'd gone to school with. That had been the main factor in their favour. But…

Were these low-lifes trying to rip her off? A pregnant woman? A *lone* pregnant woman? His hands clenched. All the tension that had eased out of him from her simple exercise shot back now.

He glanced down at the written quote. He didn't know the builder responsible for this either. He shoved his chair back and shot to his feet. 'C'mon.'

She blinked. 'C'mon, what?'

'We're going to see an old friend of mine—I went to school with him—he's a builder.' John might despise Luke now, but he wouldn't rip him off. Of that, Luke was certain. 'And we're going to drop by the agency and collect the key to *your* house.'

She didn't rise from her chair. She folded her arms and

glared. 'I'm more than capable of speaking to a builder and collecting the key to the house myself.' Her glare lost its force. 'I would appreciate the name of a builder you'd recommend, though.'

For a moment he considered leaving her to it. This wasn't his problem. No skin off his nose. He didn't *want* to get involved. But her face that night at the bathroom door rose up in his mind, and he couldn't shake the thought of what would have happened to Tammy if she'd had to face her pregnancy alone.

He planted his feet. 'It'll be easier if I come along.'

'You have a farm to run.'

'It'll survive without me for an afternoon.'

'No way! You told me you're coming up to harvest.'

He'd forgotten that darn independence of hers. He could add stubborn to the mix now too. He set his jaw. 'Keira, you're only here for what—five more days?' Five days! He could count that off on the fingers of one hand. 'Local knowledge is going to be necessary in this situation.'

She bit her lip.

He pressed his advantage. 'And what if you start feeling queasy again?'

She stood too, hands on hips. Her linen trousers were all creased and wrinkled from sitting, but she still looked fresh and cool. 'If I'm to accept your help, and that help takes you away from the farm, then…then we need to come to some arrangement. Either I pay you for your time to act on my behalf—'

'No!' He wasn't taking her money. At least not for something like this. He wasn't accepting anything more from her than her rent money.

'Or I pay you in kind.'

He folded his arms. He could see she wouldn't be easy to budge. 'What did you have in mind?'

She eyed him up and down. 'It doesn't look as if you've any kind of sports injuries I can work on.'

The thought of her fingers moving over his flesh was far too tempting. And disturbing. 'Nope.' He said it quickly, before he could change his mind.

'Well…' She glanced around. 'From now until I leave I'll cook dinner every night and do some light cleaning. I know it won't make up for losing a whole afternoon's work on the farm.' She folded her arms too and lifted her chin. 'But it's something.'

To come home every evening and find her in his kitchen, cooking their meals, for the next five nights… He swallowed. Could he deal with that? If he were ready for it, expecting it, then he wouldn't lose it like he had last night, right?

'Well?'

He hated cooking. He held out his hand. 'Deal.'

She placed hers in it, and sent him the kind of smile that could blindside a man if he wasn't forewarned. Just as well he was forewarned.

He scowled and let go of her hand. Her skin was warm and soft—and so fair!

'Do you have a hat?' he barked at her. 'You shouldn't be walking around outside at this time of year without a hat.'

She blinked. 'I forgot to pack one. I'll…um…get one next time I go shopping.'

'Good. Now, let's make tracks.'

He turned and strode out of the house, not checking to see if she followed. He knew she did—he could smell her, sense her. His hands clenched. It suddenly occurred to him that forewarned didn't necessarily mean forearmed.

Keira couldn't believe how easy it was to get the key from the agency. To her utter shame, it hadn't occurred to her to request it earlier. Although she knew she had every right to the key, some inner instinct had warned her the agent would do his best to block her, find excuses for why she couldn't have it.

Nothing doing—it was a piece of cake! The receptionist took one look at Luke, and Keira swore the poor woman literally started to shake. She'd handed the key over without a murmur.

It had taken a considerable effort not to burst out laughing. So Luke obviously had a reputation for being difficult, huh? If the agency hadn't worked out yet that his bark was worse then his bite then far be it from her to set them straight. And while she was more than capable of standing up for herself—an independent woman, a strong woman following in the tradition of her mother and grandmother—she had to admit that Luke's reassuring bulk was a decided comfort.

Luke's face grew grimmer, however, when they pulled to a halt outside a long metal building. 'This is John's workshop.'

She unclipped her seatbelt. 'You said you went to school with him?'

'Yeah—John Peterson. He's a good guy. Whatever he tells us, we can take it as gospel.'

'Good.' She paused in the act of opening her door. Luke hadn't moved. 'So what are we waiting for?'

He shook himself. 'Nothing.'

She followed him into the small office at the front of the building. The whirr and buzz of machinery, hammering and sawing, sounded from beyond the partitioned wall, but the office itself was empty.

Keira reached around Luke, who stood frozen, to ring the bell. Almost immediately a barrel-chested bear of a man strode in. He stopped short when he saw Luke.

Oh, dear. Keira bit her lip. Obviously someone else who considered Luke difficult.

But then the tanned face broke into a broad grin and he

moved forward with hand outstretched. 'Luke, it's good to see you! Haven't seen your ugly mug around for a while.'

Luke looked as if he wanted to run, but he held his ground and shook the man's hand. 'Notice you haven't got any prettier since the last time I saw you, Peterson.'

The riposte looked as if it had taken John as off guard as it had her. The other man, though, just threw his head back and laughed. He clapped Luke on the back. 'What can I do for you?'

'This is Keira.' Luke ushered her forward. 'She's my… guest at the moment.'

Keira took pity on him. 'Lodger,' she explained, shaking John's hand too.

'Keira's inherited a house in town. She's been given a quote for some work that needs doing, but she'd like a second opinion.'

Luke pulled out her quote from his shirt pocket and handed it across to John. She saw the way John's lips tightened when he glanced at the letterhead. She also noted the look the two men exchanged.

'I thought you might be able to help.'

'I'd be glad to.' John glanced at his watch. 'If you aren't busy, I've half an hour to spare now…'

'That's what I was hoping you'd say.' Luke smiled. That same smile that had almost knocked her sideways off the kitchen chair earlier.

He should do that more often—smile—it made him look younger. Like thirty-three rather than close to forty, where she'd fixed him.

'Will that work for you?'

She blinked and realised he was addressing her. 'Oh, yes! That's perfect.'

She gave John the address, and they arranged to meet there in five minutes.

* * *

John crouched down to peer under the house, the beam of his flashlight stretching to the furthest reaches. He snorted. 'Who is this joker trying to kid?'

Keira knelt down beside him. 'What?'

Luke crouched down on her other side. She was too aware of him—of his heat, of the strength that rippled beneath the denim of his jeans, informing her of the powerful thigh muscles concealed beneath. Jeans that looked worn...thin... as if they might rip at any moment and give her a tantalising glimpse of flesh. She watched, holding her breath, mesmerised by his latent power, by—

'He claims that the whole house needs to be re-piered.'

She snapped to at John's words. She glanced up to find Luke watching her. His eyes darkened. Heat flooded her face, her neck. His gaze dropped to her lips. She started to sway towards him...

She snatched herself back. *Yikes!*

Luke shot to his feet.

Piers! They were talking about piers. 'So...um...they *don't* need replacing?'

'These four here—' John pointed to them with his flashlight '—could do with jacking up, but it's not urgent.'

'Well, that's good news,' she said, rising and risking another glance at Luke. His face had shuttered closed.

'Okay, let's head on inside.'

She handed John the key, and tried not to mind if Luke followed them or not.

Her great-aunt's house was an old colonial-style weatherboard. It had three generous bedrooms, high ceilings and moulded cornices, picture rails and an eat-in kitchen. Keira loved its lack of pretension and its sense of calm.

She didn't say anything, just followed John as he made his way through the house. He spent a long time surveying the kitchen.

'Okay,' he said finally, 'the kitchen and bathroom could

do with modernising, but again that's not urgent. Currently they're both serviceable.'

She digested the news silently.

Beside her, Luke stiffened. He hadn't said much of anything since John had started his inspection. After that moment outside he'd kept an ocean of distance between himself and Keira—always a room behind or a room in front. Now he opened the back door and stalked out into the yard, pacing its length. She watched him from the window above the kitchen sink and tried to pinpoint exactly what it was about the man that sang such a siren's song to her.

She snorted. Well, how about that magnificent physique for a start?

Deep down, though, she sensed it was something more than that. There was something about the way he held his head—a certain look sometimes in those dark eyes of his. And something about the way he'd mopped her face after she'd been sick, in the way he'd thrust that packet of biscuits at her before he'd stormed off to bed. He might be a tad cantankerous—or a lot, she admitted—but beneath all that gruffness he hid a kind heart.

'I don't know what you did,' John said, joining her at the window, 'but I want to thank you. It's good to see Luke out and about again.'

'What do you mean?' She forced her gaze from the man pacing the backyard. 'I haven't done anything. Except be a nuisance.'

'You've taken his mind off his own misery—for a bit at least. These last few years he's buried himself away at Candlebark and hardly ever emerges.'

Really? Luke was a hermit? She frowned. 'That's…um… taking the workaholic thing a bit far.'

John nodded out of the window. 'He's been through a rough time, whatever anyone says. Don't you go paying attention to small town gossip, you hear? People can be vicious. Luke—he's a good guy.'

'Yeah, I know.'

She frowned again. What small-town gossip? What were people saying about Luke? And why?

She turned from locking the front door to her great-aunt's house, and the three of moved towards their cars. 'So,' Keira said, 'everything this builder Mr Selway has recommended is nonsense?'

John nodded.

She sucked her bottom lip into her mouth. 'Is that legal?'

'It'd be hard to prove,' he said carefully, coming to a halt beside his truck. 'There's little doubt that if he did everything he says on your quote it would add value to the house. I'd say it was overcapitalising, but if you tried to challenge him about misleading you he could simply claim that you misunderstood—that he wasn't saying it *had* to be done, only that it would improve the property.'

Right. 'But...you're not convinced he *would* do everything listed on my quote, are you?' she said slowly. 'You think he means to charge me the earth for doing next to nothing?'

'That's my guess. But I can't prove it.'

Beside her, she was aware of Luke opening and closing his fists, as if readying himself to punch something. 'And both of you also think this Mr Selway and Mr Connors, my estate agent, are in this together—don't you?'

John nodded. 'What's more, I'll make an educated guess that your solicitor is Graeme Aldershot.'

Her jaw dropped.

'He and Selway went to school together. When Connors arrived from the city they all became very buddy-buddy.'

The grooves either side of Luke's mouth deepened. 'I'll be having a word with Connors first thing.'

John flexed an arm. '*I'll* be having a word with Selway first thing.'

Keira planted her hands on her hips. 'Excellent. I have an appointment with Mr Aldershot tomorrow. I mean to tell him that I'm considering pressing charges against Selway and Connors. Not that I am—I don't need the hassle—but he doesn't need to know that. I won't let on that I know he's part of it all, and I'll ask him to represent me.' She dusted off her hands.

John threw his head back and laughed. 'Good for you, Keira. That should put the fear of God into him.'

She hoped so.

John held out his hand. 'It was nice meeting you.'

'Likewise—and thank you.' She'd drop around to his workshop tomorrow with a nice bottle of single-malt Scotch. He'd certainly earned it.

'Great to see you, Luke.'

Luke clapped him on the shoulder. 'Thanks for all your help. I appreciate it. Ever need a favour in return...'

John nodded and climbed into his truck. Keira lifted her hand in farewell as it pulled away, before turning back to survey her great-aunt's house. 'It's nice, isn't it?' Homey. She could imagine a family living there—growing into it and loving it.

Luke leant on the ute beside her. 'Yeah, it is. You won't have any trouble selling it. Especially with the park across the road.'

It *was* a pretty location. A child's paradise. It was the kind of house that if she saw it in the city and could afford it she'd snap up in an instant. A muffled weight settled over her shoulders. She didn't know why selling the house should make her feel sad—except perhaps that it was the only link she had to a part of her family she'd never known. The last of her family.

Now that she was pregnant, family had started taking on

a whole new dimension for her, and at odd moments its lack filled her with nameless fears. What if she died as young as her mother? Who would love and care for her child?

She knew it was pointless fretting about such what-ifs. She had friends who'd be more than happy to step into the breach. But it wasn't the same as being able to rely on family.

She turned to the man beside her. 'Do you have a large family, Luke?'

He stared out to the front, his eyes narrowed as if against the glare of the sun—only the sun was behind them. 'Not really.'

She waited. Nothing. 'Parents?'

'Yeah, but they retired to the coast nearly three years ago now.'

She digested that. Then stiffened. Tammy had died three years ago, hadn't she? Luke and Tammy might no longer have lived together, but surely Luke's parents would have stuck around to help Luke and Jason through such a terrible time?

She swallowed. 'Siblings?'

'An older brother—Evan. He married an English girl and emigrated.'

'So...none of you are close, then?'

He glanced down at her. 'We're not at loggerheads or anything.'

She'd never considered herself short, at five feet five inches, but Luke dwarfed her. She didn't want to find that so deliciously appealing, but she did. She didn't want to lean into him and gain strength from his mere presence, his very solidity.

Liar!

Well, okay...yes, she did. She wanted *that* a lot. But she didn't want to want it.

Don't get too used to relying on this man, she warned herself. She couldn't risk relying on anyone too much at present. She had to focus on her pregnancy and creating a wonderful life for her baby. In eighteen months, two years—maybe then she'd be ready to let someone into their lives, but not yet.

'My mother called me her change of life baby.'

Keira swung back in time to see him pass a hand through his hair. He smelt of dirt and grease and fresh-mown grass. Not one of those smells made her stomach churn, or had perspiration emerging as she tried to combat nausea. In fact she found herself kind of liking the way he smelled. It was refreshing after the heavy colognes of some of her friends in the city.

'I came along when she was forty-six and my father fifty-three. Evan was already grown up at twenty-four.'

Wow! 'It must've been hard, being the lone child among all those adults?'

'It was all right.'

And that was when she saw it—as if he'd spoken the words out loud. Luke had felt like an intruder in his own family. She didn't know what sixth sense had suddenly fired to life inside her, making her see him so clearly. She didn't know what part of her could be so finely attuned to that same part of him, but her heart started to ache for the little boy he must once have been.

No wonder he'd searched for love with Tammy when he was only nineteen.

She slipped her arm though his and hugged it. He glanced down in surprise, but didn't detach himself. 'Thank you for helping me out today. You've saved me thousands of dollars and months of delay.'

'You saved yourself. You were the one who sensed something wasn't right.' His hands clenched. 'I'm glad you did! I'm sorry you were almost taken advantage of like that.'

Beneath her hand, the muscles in his arms tightened. She rubbed her hand up and down it to ease the tension, dug her fingers into the muscle to find the knots and loosen them. 'It wasn't your fault.'

He scowled. 'What a great opinion you'll have of our country hospitality now.'

He glanced down at her hands, and she realised she'd started a full-blown massage on his arm. She leapt away. 'Sorry.' She coughed to hide her confusion, shoved her hands into her back pockets. 'Force of habit.'

He didn't move for a moment, but then one corner of his mouth kicked up. He lifted a shoulder. 'There are worse habits to have.'

Her heart jumped and jerked. Her knees wobbled. 'I… um…my opinion of country hospitality could take an upward swing if you wouldn't mind dropping in at the supermarket on our way home.'

His smile faded.

'Don't worry about it,' she rushed on. Of course he had work he wanted to get to. 'I can come back into town later.'

He shrugged again, but his tension belied the studied casualness. 'We're here now. I'm figuring it won't take long?'

'No time at all. I just want to grab some things for dinner.'

When they entered the supermarket, Luke scanned the crowd. Keira watched and waited. After a moment his shoulders unhitched a notch, and he insisted on pushing the shopping trolley for her. She let out a breath she hadn't realised she'd held, and handed the trolley over wordlessly.

She sped through the shop as quickly as she could, aware that Luke probably had a million things to do and not wanting to hold him up longer than she had to.

She dropped the last thing in the trolley. 'There—that's it. Now we can make for the checkouts.' And home.

But when she turned she found her path blocked. 'Oh, I'm sorry.'

She moved to one side, to let the woman pass, but the woman followed her. And then she pushed her face in close to Keira's. 'I hope you know what it is you're doing!' she hissed.

Keira backed up, but the trolley behind brought her up short. The woman was probably in her mid-sixties, and she was grey, drawn, thin. Everything about her was faded except her eyes, which flashed with sparks of bitter green fury.

'That man you're with—you know he's a monster? That he's a heartless murderer!'

CHAPTER FOUR

'GRAN, don't.'

Keira blinked. 'Jason!'

Jason stood beside the woman, his eyes downcast. Keira tried to pick her jaw up. This was…Tammy's mother? And she blamed Luke for Tammy's death? Bile rose in her throat. Luke was no murderer. She knew that as surely as she knew her own name.

'Gran, this is Keira. She's renting our room.'

The pleading in Jason's voice caught at Keira's heart. He might as well have saved himself the bother, though. His grandmother's venom had already moved from Keira to the man standing behind her.

'Hello, Brenda,' Luke said quietly. Those grooves either side of his mouth deepened. His skin had turned grey.

'How on earth can you bear to show your face in this town? I *spit* on you, Luke Hillier!'

Thankfully she didn't literally put the threat into action, but her words made Luke pale even further. His jaw had set so hard Keira feared for it. She remembered what John had told her about the viciousness of small-town gossip and acid burned her stomach.

'C'mon, love…'

A man—Jason's grandfather, Keira guessed—sent Luke a glare of loathing before leading his wife away. Jason stared from them to his father in anguish. Keira's heart broke for him. She touched his arm and tried to smile. 'Would you like a ride home?'

He glanced up at his father. 'Uh…yeah.'

'I'll wait for you both in the car. You'll carry the groceries for Keira?' Luke said.

'Yeah, sure.'

Keira's heart broke for Luke as he strode away too.

She turned back to Jason, took in his school uniform. 'It's a bit early for school to be out, isn't it?'

'Last day of term,' he mumbled. 'There was an assembly.'

'Right.' She didn't need to ask why Luke hadn't attended. That reason had become startlingly and horrifyingly clear.

'I'm sorry…' he shuffled his feet '…'bout all that.'

'Oh, Jason, it's not your fault.'

His face twisted. 'Then whose fault *is* it? Dad's? Gran's and Grandad's?'

'I'm not sure it's anyone's fault.'

She manoeuvred the trolley to a nearby checkout. Jason started unloading the groceries. Keira didn't try to help. She didn't remonstrate at his rough handling of the vegetables or eggs. She sensed he needed something to do with his hands. Though he did his best to hide it his agitation was evident, and she wanted to do whatever she could to soothe it.

'People react in different ways when they lose someone they love. Sometimes in irrational ways.'

'But—'

He broke off, as if he'd been about to say something and then thought better of it. She didn't press him. '*My* mum died when I was fourteen.'

He spun to stare at that. 'Yeah?'

'It was awful—the worst time of my life. You know all about that, though.'

He shrugged and nodded. He didn't back away from her as he had up until now.

'But I can't imagine how awful it would be to lose a child. It's the wrong order, you see. Children are supposed to outlive their parents.'

Jason's brow creased. 'So you think it might be harder for Gran and Grandad to accept that...that Mum's gone than anyone else?'

'Maybe.'

'They hate Dad.'

Keira swallowed. That had been all too evident.

'They say that because they'd separated and weren't living together any more that proves he didn't love Mum.'

How on earth could his grandparents do this to him—tear his loyalties like this? She did her best to keep her voice even. 'I think there must be more than a hundred different kinds of love in the world. Just because your mum and dad weren't living together any more it doesn't mean they'd stopped caring about each other. What do you think?'

Jason scuffed the toe of one sneaker against the floor. 'Dunno.'

'Have you tried talking to your dad about it?'

He glanced away. She recalled how shuttered and closed-off Luke could be, and grimaced. She wasn't sure if she'd be brave enough to broach the subject if she were Jason, either.

She paid for the groceries and went to lift her share of the bags, but Jason beat her to it. 'Dad told me to carry them,' he muttered.

For a moment he so reminded her of Luke that her lips twitched. She straightened, placed her hands on her hips. 'Did your dad tell you that I'm pregnant?' She didn't mind if he had. It wasn't a secret. She'd already spread the news far and wide among her friends.

Jason's jaw dropped. He stared at her stomach. 'Are you?'

'Yep.'

His eyes lit up. 'Sweet!'

'I think so.'

He grinned. It stunned her. She hadn't seen him grin before, and it transformed him completely. It caught the awkwardness of his age perfectly—trapped somewhere between childhood and adulthood. It brought all her maternal urges rushing to the surface, turning her to mush.

'Am I supposed to offer you my arm or something?' he said, mock gallant, but grinning like an idiot.

Laughter spurted out of her. 'Try it and I'll box your ears.'

That was when it occurred to her that what Luke and Jason needed was a bit of fun in their lives.

Luke couldn't believe it. When Keira and Jason emerged from the supermarket they were...*laughing*!

Keira had obviously told Jason she was pregnant, because all the way back to Candlebark they tossed around babies' names, of all things. As if that incident in the supermarket had never happened.

The ute didn't have a back seat, so they all had to ride in the front. Keira sat in the middle. Every now and again the movement of the car had her shoulder brushing his. Each and every time a wave of vanilla would engulf him.

The scent didn't soothe him. It attacked all his nerve-endings, fraying them with a relentless reminder of all he'd turned his back on, of a life he could never have—a life that held softness and sweetness and bone-deep contentment.

He'd turned all those things to dust for Tammy, and every time he saw Brenda and Alf it was like a scab being ripped off an old wound. He deserved their hate and censure, but *they* deserved to find some peace. Every time he saw them guilt swallowed him whole because he knew they hadn't found it.

And seeing him only made it worse for them.

He bit back an oath. It was why he avoided going into town wherever possible—to try and spare them at least that much. And look where his Good Samaritan act had landed him today!

From the corner of his eye he glanced at Keira. No matter how hard he tried, he couldn't find it in him to regret helping her.

'What do you reckon, Dad?'

Luke shook himself. 'Sorry?'

'What's your favourite name for a girl? In case that's what Keira has?'

He didn't know why Jason was so fascinated by Keira's pregnancy. 'I...dunno.' He shrugged. It was nothing to him.

'Well, what if it's a boy, then?' Jason persisted.

Luke wanted out of the cab of the ute—fast. He turned into the driveway at Candlebark, eased his foot off the accelerator when what he really wanted to do was floor it.

'Well?'

'Uh...Jason.' He latched onto that. 'Jason is a good name for a boy.'

He pulled the ute to a halt by the barn.

'What other names did you and Mum have picked out?'

The question froze Luke's blood. 'I can't remember.' He shot out of the car. 'Got work to do!' he fired over his shoulder.

'Need a hand?' Jason called after him.

Luke shook his head and kept walking.

When Luke pushed through the back door that evening he stumbled to a halt, half frozen in the act of hauling off his hat and dragging his forearm across his brow.

Someone had stolen his kitchen.

And replaced it with a picture of domestic bliss. He blinked. The scene didn't waver and disappear. He tried to raise Brenda and Alf's faces to his mind, to temper the gratitude that raced through him—he didn't deserve this—but that didn't work either.

Keira stood by the stove. Jason sat at the table chatting to her. The table was laid with a red and green checked cloth and the cutlery shone. A glass bowl of salad sat in the middle of the table, and Keira now turned to set a bowl of warmed rolls beside it. She sent him one of those trademarks smiles of hers, and the weight of the afternoon lifted from him.

'You're just in time.'

He nodded. He didn't trust himself to speak.

And then she leant down and pulled a lasagne from the oven. It looked great. It smelled even better. His mouth started to water. 'Did you make that?'

'She did.' Jason shook his head in awe. 'From scratch!'

Luke washed his hands and took his seat. He dragged the scents that filled the kitchen into his lungs. He savoured the way his shoulders and arms ached from the afternoon's hard digging.

Keira set a plate of lasagne in front of him, and he wondered if she knew how lovely she looked with damp tendrils clinging to her neck and around her temples. She'd scraped her hair up into some kind of topknot, obviously to keep it out of the way while she'd been preparing the food. Her skin had a healthy rosy glow. She looked good enough to eat.

'What?' She touched a hand to her face. 'Do I have tomato paste on my face or something?'

He yanked himself around. 'No, I...uh...this looks great.'

He couldn't remember the last time he and Jason had sat at the table and had a meal together. He touched his knife, fingered the tablecloth. They'd used to eat together in the lounge room, with the television on, but somewhere along the way Jason had gravitated towards the computer in the evenings and Luke had holed up in his study to keep on top of the farm accounts.

'It's the least I could do after all your help today.'

'Keira told me what you did,' Jason piped up. 'That was pretty cool, Dad.'

Luke couldn't remember the last time Jason had paid him any kind of compliment either. And it felt good.

In fact it felt great.

Keira must have noticed the way he fiddled with the table-cloth, because she said, 'I found it in the linen press. I hope you don't mind?'

'No.'

She took her seat too. 'It seemed kind of Christmassy, and as it *is* the season to be jolly and all...'

Luke didn't answer. In all honesty he'd forgotten it was Christmas.

'Tuck in,' she said. 'Help yourselves to salad and rolls. Eat up while it's still hot.'

Neither he nor Jason needed any further encouragement.

'So,' she said after a bit, 'what do you guys do for Christmas?'

He shrugged. 'Nothing.' Jason usually spent Christmas with Tammy's parents. 'It's just another day around here.'

Her cutlery clattered back to her plate. 'What do you mean? You take the day off, don't you?'

'Nope.'

'But...but don't you have a special meal, and exchange gifts, and play Christmas carols and charades and pull Christmas crackers?'

Luke shook his head. Since Tammy had died they hadn't had the heart for Christmas.

Luke's forkful of lasagne halted halfway to his mouth when he saw Jason staring at Keira with a kind of enthralled fascination. 'What do *you* do?' his son asked.

Keira picked up her knife and fork again. 'There's a group of my friends and we've dubbed ourselves The Orphans. Not that we all are, mind, but those of us who don't have family, or who can't visit them for Christmas, all get together for a big seafood buffet. We eat too much, play silly games, and just generally have a rowdy old time.'

'That sounds…kinda cool.'

Luke stared at him. It did?

'It is.'

He tried to ignore the glare she sent him.

'Keira was sick this afternoon,' Jason suddenly announced.

'Ooh, traitor!' She pointed her fork at him.

'She said it's normal. Is it?'

'Yeah, sometimes,' Luke assured him. He surveyed Keira through narrowed eyes. 'How are you feeling now?'

'Very well, thank you. I had a nice cup of liquorice tea and it settled my stomach nicely.'

'Keira said you were the one who put her onto that?'

Luke ran a finger beneath the collar of his T-shirt. Was the darn woman set on becoming the all-dancing, all-singing president of his fan club or something? He grunted. 'It was nothing.' He shovelled the last of his lasagne down. The domesticity in the kitchen was starting to wrap around him too tightly.

'Did Mum have morning sickness?'

The lasagne threatened to rise again. Luke swallowed hard. 'For a bit.'

'Would you like seconds?' Keira asked, sending him one of those shiny smiles of hers.

She half rose, but he shook his head. His appetite had fled.

Jason suddenly burst out with, 'Were you and Mum as happy about having a baby as Keira is?'

Luke tried to stop his jaw from dropping. Ice streaked from his scalp down to the soles of his feet. He didn't have the energy, the strength…the *heart* for this. 'Keira's carefully planned becoming pregnant. Of course she's happy to find out that that all her hard work hasn't been for nothing.'

Jason scowled, the familiar surly teenager re-emerging. 'And I wasn't planned.' It was a statement, not a question.

What on earth...? Jason already knew all this. Luke pushed out of his chair. 'We were nineteen. We were petrified.'

He couldn't stand remembering that time—the mistakes he'd made...the miscalculations.

Without another word he strode out through the door and into the gathering darkness.

Keira stared in disbelief as the door slammed shut behind Luke. She turned back to the scowling teenager and swallowed. Was Luke deliberately trying to alienate his son?

'You know,' she started, 'if I'd fallen pregnant at nineteen I'd have been petrified too.'

Jason didn't say anything. He shoved away from the table and stalked off. Keira slumped in her chair. To think she'd thought a nice, cosy dinner would be just the thing...

Luke sat bolt upright in bed and listened, staring intently into the dark.

Was Keira was being sick again?

In the next moment his suspicions were confirmed. He hauled himself out of bed and pulled on his trusty tracksuit pants.

The bathroom door opened before he could knock.

'Oh, Luke!' She pulled up short and tried to smile. 'We've got to stop meeting like this.'

His stomach clenched. She looked ghastly—a sickly pale grey, with fine lines fanning out from her eyes and mouth, and a film of perspiration clinging to her forehead and top lip. Her attempt at a joke kicked him in the gut. He didn't know where she found the strength. Or the courage.

'I'm sorry—I didn't mean to disturb you. Go back to bed. I'm fine again now.'

He took one look at the way she leaned against the door-jamb, as if in need of its support. He slipped an arm around her waist. 'C'mon, we'll make you a cup of something hot. Don't argue,' he added, when she lifted a hand as if to remonstrate with him. 'I'm awake now.'

Her soft weight tucked in against his side as if it belonged there, making him want to pull her closer. The scent of vanilla clung to her hair and he wanted to bury his face in it. Hormones long buried, urges long denied, clamoured to the surface, racing through him with a speed and insistence that made his heart pound. When she laid a hand against his bare chest to steady herself, he thought he might lose the plot altogether.

Get a grip! She's ill. Had he sunk so low he'd take advantage of a sick woman?

No!

But this temptation had been building all day. He'd wanted to touch her from the moment he'd found her rifling though his sideboard. At her great-aunt's place he'd nearly kissed her! She'd turned and looked up at him with those big grey eyes of hers and he'd wanted to seize her face in his hands and slant his lips over hers.

He gritted his teeth and helped her into a chair at the kitchen table, then backed away. 'Liquorice tea or lemon?'

'Lemon, please.'

Kissing Keira was out of the question. He couldn't tarnish this lovely woman with his indefensible irresponsibility, his sinister and inexplicable inconstancy. To dim her wide smiles and all her colour, her bright hopes for the future, would be unforgivable.

'Thank you,' she murmured when he set a steaming mug in front of her.

She closed her eyes and took a sip. Luke stared, fascinated at the way her lips shaped themselves to the mug. With an oath, he kicked himself away to pull a packet of plain biscuits from the pantry. 'You should try to eat something.' He hooked out the chair opposite and planted himself in it, gripped his hands together so they wouldn't do anything stupid.

'Maybe in a bit,' she said, with a tiny shake of her head.

He suspected she didn't want to risk any larger, more vigorous movements. He should go back to bed, put himself out of temptation's way. Even as the thought drifted into his mind he knew he wouldn't act on it. He couldn't leave her like this when she was still so unwell. What if she fainted?

His hands clenched. What if she fainted when she returned to the city and there was no one to pick her up from the floor and put her to bed?

'I'd have been petrified if I'd fallen pregnant at nineteen too,' she said, apropos of nothing.

He stiffened.

'Sometimes I get terrified now, and I planned my baby.'

His back unbent again. 'What do you get scared about?'

'The usual stuff, I suppose.' One slender shoulder lifted. 'Will I be a good mum? Can I do it on my own? Will my baby hate growing up without a father and blame me for the decisions I've made?' She paused. 'The worst one, though, is what will happen to my child if I die as young as my mother?'

His gut clenched. Everything inside him rebelled at the thought.

'I worry that the cancer my mother had could be hereditary, and what if I pass that on to my baby?' She shook her head. 'I know it's silly to brood about things outside of my control, but...'

But it didn't make her fears any less real. 'What happened to you after your mother died?'

'My gran looked after me. She'd always lived with us.'

'Your grandmother didn't die young?'

'Well...no.'

'So maybe you and your baby will take after her.'

Keira stared at him. And then she smiled—a bull's-eye of a smile. 'I hadn't thought of that!'

He angled the packet of biscuits towards her. She took one, nibbled a corner. 'So you were scared about becoming a dad?'

'Sure.' He took a biscuit too, to give him something to do with his hands and in the hope it would distract him from the intriguing mobility of her face.

She stared at him for a moment. She put her biscuit down. 'What was it like the first time Jason was placed in your arms?'

He sat back and rewound his memories nearly fifteen years. He remembered the awe and the all-consuming love that had slammed into him. Jason had been so tiny and perfect. 'It was…magic.'

'Then why didn't you tell Jason that at dinnertime?'

Because it would have meant remembering how things had been, and how it had all then gone pear-shaped. And how that was his fault.

He had to live with that knowledge every day. Wasn't that enough?

'Don't you want a better relationship with your son?'

'There's nothing wrong with my relationship with Jason!'

She frowned. 'You can't honestly believe that?'

Her incredulity stung. 'Jason knows he wasn't planned, but he knows Tammy and I loved him.'

'Are you so sure of that?'

'What makes you think I'm wrong?' he shot back.

'The look on Jason's face when you stormed out this evening.'

He swore. His hand clenched to a fist, crushing the half-eaten biscuit.

That cute little furrow of hers etched itself into the centre of her forehead. 'Are you deliberately trying to push him away?'

'What are you talking about?' He was doing no such thing. He tried to concentrate on ridding himself of the crumbs.

'You won't let him help out on the farm whenever he offers. You won't talk to him about his childhood.' She paused and speared him with a glance. 'You won't talk to him about Tammy.'

He flinched at that last. So? What did that prove? What did she know? Nothing! 'He doesn't need to bother about the farm. That's my responsibility. I want him to hang out with his friends after school and on the weekends—relax, have fun.'

'He doesn't, though, Luke. He shuts himself up in his bedroom. On his own. He's becoming as big a hermit as you.'

Her words sucker-punched him. He stared at her, slack-jawed.

'He *wants* to help out with the farm chores.'

'Why?' The word croaked out of him.

Her eyes softened. 'Because he wants to hang out with you.'

All the strength seeped from his spine.

'And, Luke, you might want to save him from responsibility and the demands of the farm for as long as you can, but it's not going to make up for losing his mum. Even if it does make you feel better.'

Was that what he'd been doing? Trying to atone for the unpardonable, the unforgivable? Was he trying to ease his conscience at the expense of his son? The thought appalled him. He thought he'd been protecting Jason. But…was he only hurting him more?

Luke couldn't stand that thought. He'd lay his life down for his son, do anything to protect him from harm.

He'd have laid his life down for Tammy too, if he'd been given the chance, but life rarely allowed you to make those kinds of bargains. He didn't doubt for one moment that Jason would have been a million times better off if his and Tammy's situations had been reversed.

And now here was this woman who'd been at Candlebark for all of three days and it seemed she knew more about his son than he did.

'You forget,' she said softly, 'that I lost my mother when I was young too. I can guess at, relate to, some of the things Jason is feeling.'

If he were a better father, he would have been able to guess at them too.

'Why won't you talk about Tammy with him and tell him about the things you all used to do when he was little?'

'Why does he need me to talk about that stuff?' The very idea made him go cold all over. Brenda and Alf—they talked to Jason about Tammy all the time. It wasn't as if he was missing out.

She didn't say anything for a long moment. 'You want to know one of the things that scared me most after Mum died?'

He ran his hand through his hair. She'd said her mum had died ten years ago. Fourteen was too young to lose your mum. And she hadn't had a dad. He wanted to get up and walk away, but he couldn't. 'What?'

'That I'd start to forget her. That I'd forget what she looked like and smelt like and the sound of her voice. That the memories would fade.'

Jason forget his mum? He stiffened. 'He'll never forget Tammy!'

'I know that, and you know that. But only you and Tammy's parents stand between Jason and that fear. And, forgive me for saying so, but I doubt he's getting much…balance…from his grandparents. He's a smart kid. He'll know that.'

Luke recalled the stoic eleven-year-old who'd watched his mother's coffin lowered into the ground. If their situations had been reversed, Tammy would have known what Jason needed.

Instead Jason was stuck with a father who didn't have a clue. 'What helped you get through that?'

Keira glanced about the kitchen. 'Why aren't there any photographs of Tammy around?'

He closed his eyes. 'Tammy and I had been living in the city. When we moved back to Gunnedah—' because it was what *he'd* wanted '—we never got around to unpacking a lot of our boxes.' Then they'd separated. And then she'd fallen sick. In the end it had been too hard to go through that stuff.

For him. It hit him now. Not for Jason. 'I'll dig some photos out—put them around.' They'd reproach him every single day, but it was no more than he deserved.

'Jason would love to help you.'

He nodded heavily. 'Right.'

Keira stared at him for a moment. 'Talking about my mum with Gran kept her alive for me. Hearing my grandma and my mother's friends talk about her made me...' Her face grew sad, wistful and even more beautiful.

'Made you what?'

'Happy,' she finally said. 'It made me happy to know that people remembered her and still loved her and understood what the world had lost when she died.' She reddened, pulled back and smoothed down her hair. 'If that makes any kind of sense,' she mumbled.

'It makes perfect sense.' And for a moment, when she smiled, the heaviness left him.

It crashed back down a moment later when she said, 'Talking about Tammy—would it be so hard to do?'

He unlocked his jaw. 'Mine and Tammy's marriage...it didn't last. I let her down. How on earth do I explain that to Jason?'

'Oh, Luke! You and Tammy were nineteen when you married?'

He nodded.

'And you married because she was pregnant?'

He nodded again.

'Then tell Jason the truth. That you were too young. That you married for the wrong reasons, but with the best intentions in the world.'

There was so much more to it than that—a whole lot more...

'Did you ever cheat on Tammy, Luke? Were you ever cruel to her?'

'No!'

'And did you ever make her feel guilty for marrying you?'

His head snapped back. 'No!' How could she even *think* that? Tammy had had nothing to feel guilty about. She'd had a heart as big as Keira's. He should have been able to love her the way she'd wanted him to.

'And you still wished her well after you separated?'

'Hell, yes! She...she was my best friend.'

'Then tell Jason *that* too. Luke, you have nothing to reproach yourself for.'

Yes, he did.

That weight settled around him more firmly—making it hard to move, hard to talk...hard to think. He'd caused Tammy so much pain—what if he did that to his son?

Maybe keeping his distance was the smartest thing to do—the best thing for Jason? He knew Brenda and Alf tried to poison Jason against him. And why not? They were probably more right than not. He knew they pressed Jason to live with them. Every day he expected Jason to announce that was exactly what he meant to do. He steeled himself for it. Dreaded it.

'Luke?'

He glanced up.

'Given all that you know now—that you would be left to bring up Jason alone—do you wish you and Tammy had never had him?'

CHAPTER FIVE

'No!' HOW could she think that of him? He loved his son. 'I could never wish Jason away. I cannot regret having him.' He might regret marrying Tammy, but he could never regret his son.

'Even though it's hard?'

Hard? Some days it was hell. His hands curled into fists. 'Yes.'

'And a struggle?'

'Yes.'

She folded her arms. 'So it's hard, and it's a struggle, but you don't regret your son?'

He didn't know where she was going with this. 'That's right.'

'And you like your farm? You think this is a good place to raise Jason?'

Something unhitched in him at that question. 'That's right.' He loved this place. Returning here was the one thing he'd got right. But, heck, the farm needed work, and money—lots of money—spent on it to bring it up to scratch. That thing hitched up inside him again.

She leant towards him. 'Then where's the joy?'

Joy? With Tammy dead? Had she lost her mind?

She reached out and poked him in the shoulder. 'You've forgotten how to have fun.'

He didn't have time for fun.

'You've forgotten to be grateful for the blessings you do have. You have a son who is healthy and…and lovely.'

That almost surprised a laugh out of him. What he wouldn't give to see the look on Jason's face if he heard himself being described as *lovely*.

'And you have a beautiful place to live. You have more than a lot of people yet all you can do is scowl and frown and… and yell at people and swear!'

His jaw dropped.

'Name me three things you've liked about your day today, Luke.'

His mind went blank.

'I'll go first, shall I? One—I finally got to see my great-aunt's house and it's…it's really lovely.'

She was lovely. And off limits.

'Two—I found out that I don't have to spend thousands of dollars on said house.'

Yeah, but that didn't change the fact that someone had tried to take advantage of her.

'And three—I bought a pregnancy magazine today, and do you know my Munchkin is now about the size of a tennis ball?'

Yeah, but it was making her throw up at every available opportunity.

'Oh, and four—I also bought three pairs of the most gorgeous knitted booties at the women's auxiliary stall. They're too cute for words.' She folded her arms. 'Now it's your turn.'

His mind went blank. All he could bring to mind were Jason's burning questions at dinnertime. And the hatred and grief in Brenda and Alf's eyes.

He pushed his chair back. 'It's late. It's time we were both back in bed.' But as soon as he rose the colour that had started to steal back into Keira's face drained out again. Perspiration beaded her upper lip. Her hands trembled.

It happened in the blink of an eye.

She chanced to glance up, and he knew she could tell he'd recognised the impending signs. Somehow through it all, though, she managed a smile. Not one of those big, bright, blind-siding numbers, this one was more muted, but the simple courage behind it touched him more than anything else she could have done.

'You go back to bed, Luke. I will be fine. Thousands before me have lived through this and survived—as no doubt will thousands after me.'

He wasn't leaving her to face this on her own.

'You're not going to go, are you?' she groaned.

'No.'

'Then you'll have to excuse me,' she muttered. 'For what it's worth, as you've already seen me at my worst.'

With that, she promptly moved to the floor, braced her back against one of the kitchen cupboards, and stuck her head between her knees. Luke wanted to reach out and cradle her in his arms until she felt better.

He didn't have the right.

She wouldn't thank him for it.

Do something useful!

He racked his brain, and then retrieved the first aid kit, along with two dried kidney beans from a packet in the pantry. He sat down beside her. 'Hold out your arm.'

She did—straight out in front of her. She didn't ask any questions, and just for a moment his lips twitched. She'd make up for that later. He didn't doubt that for a moment. The reminder that the only reason she wasn't asking questions was because she felt so sick had his smile disappearing before it could form.

He turned her arm over, pressed one bean against the pressure point of her forearm about ten centimetres from her wrist, and wrapped a bandage around it to hold it in place. He repeated the process with her other arm.

She lifted her head and rested it back against the cupboard. Luke moistened a cloth and held it against her forehead. 'I'm sorry,' she whispered.

'There's nothing to apologise for.'

'Nobody warned me I'd feel this awful. I…I mean if somebody burst through the door with an axe and threatened to chop my head off I don't think I could even put up a fight.' All this was said with her eyes still closed.

'Well, for tonight at least I promise to take care of all axe murderers.'

That managed to put a faint smile on her face. It disappeared a moment later. She opened her eyes. 'Luke, what am I going to do if I ever feel this sick after I've had my baby?'

Her lovely eyes filled with tears. It kicked him in the guts. 'You'll manage amazing feats once you have a baby, Keira, I promise. And you'll have friends you can call on, and neighbours, and a babysitter you've trained up—some maternal, middle-aged mother hen—' Gunnedah abounded with those '—who'll love your baby almost as much as you do.'

'Yeah?'

'It'll work out just fine—you'll see. Now, no more talking. Close your eyes and focus on your breathing.'

'You could keep talking,' she murmured.

There was something in the way she said it that caught at him. He glanced down, but she'd obediently closed her eyes. Slowly, he removed the cloth. He'd keep talking if it helped, but…what did he talk about?'

'Tell me those three good things about your day—three things you're grateful for.'

One side of his mouth kicked up. She was irrepressible. Not to mention persistent. 'Three good things…' he said, playing for time. 'Uh…one—I had a great dinner cooked for me.' Until all that talk about Tammy it *had* been great. The food had been spectacular.

'Lasagne is my signature dish,' she whispered. 'You'd better lower your expectations for tonight.'

'I'll be grateful for anything you cook.' He'd definitely received the better part of the deal they'd made. He rushed on, because he wanted her to rest and not talk. 'Two—I got to help you out today a little, and make sure you didn't get ripped off.'

'Help a lot, you mean.'

Her voice had gained in strength, but she still kept her eyes closed. Her lashes were fair—the same red-gold as her hair—but they were long, and they rested against her cheeks in a curling sweep that he wanted to trace with a fingertip. He curled his fingers into his hands and held them in his lap.

'How was it to see John after so long?'

The question took him off-guard. He'd had to brace himself for the meeting, but he and John had fallen into their old pattern as if it the last three years had never happened. 'It was... good.' And he meant it.

'I don't really understand what's going on, but you can't honestly believe the things Tammy's parents accuse you of?'

Not literally, perhaps. But Brenda had sensed his doubt and he deserved her scorn.

'John doesn't believe a word of it.'

She was right, he realised. Today had proved that.

'I bet there are more like him in the town too.'

Could she be right?

'What's your third thing?'

He floundered for a moment, trying to come up with something. Then it hit him. 'Jason paid me a compliment at dinner.'

Her eyes opened. 'That's nice.' And then she smiled. All her colour had returned. She held her arms out to inspect them. 'Of course—pressure points. Thank you.'

'You're welcome.'

'Are you angry with me for the things I said earlier about Jason?'

He had been angry, but he could see now that his anger had been directed at himself, not her. 'I'm not angry with you, Keira.' And with that admission came the realisation he wanted to fight for his son, whatever the cost to himself.

'I thought maybe I ought to apologise.'

He shook his head. 'You've held a mirror up to me, and I can't say I much like what I see.'

'You should smile a bit more, and you shouldn't cut yourself off from your friends, but…I like what I see.'

And, although he knew it wasn't what she meant, he suddenly noticed how her nightshirt had shucked up to reveal a tantalising length of thigh. He dragged his gaze away, clenched his hands tighter, and rested his head against the cupboard behind. 'I don't want Jason becoming a hermit. That means setting him a better example.'

'Luke, you're kind and generous to lone pregnant women in distress. You fight a fair fight, you'd never cheat someone, and you work hard. I think you're the perfect example. With Jason, all you need to do is talk to him—you'll see.'

He turned his head to meet her gaze. Her eyes had gone liquid warm. It filled him with corresponding warmth. He reached out and touched her face. 'So young…so wise,' he murmured.

Her skin was soft, and her breath hitched when he traced the contour of her cheek with his fingertip. Her eyes darkened, desire flaring in their depths. An answering flame flared to life inside him. He turned to cup her cheek more fully, to tip up her chin. Her lips parted, her gaze fastened on his lips, and the pulse at the base of her throat beat like a wild thing.

He started to lower his mouth, his mind blanked of everything except the way she lifted her face to his, how her lips parted, filling him with an anticipation that had the blood roaring in his ears.

'Oh!' She pressed her fingers to his mouth with a groan just seconds before his lips could claim hers. For a brief moment she rested her forehead there. 'Bad idea,' he heard her whisper. 'Very bad idea.'

She was right, of course.

In the ordinary course of events he'd have disentangled himself and stormed off, flaying himself for so completely forgetting his resolutions. But he didn't know if sudden movements would make her nausea return, and although he knew he'd flay himself for his weakness later, he didn't have the energy for anger at that moment either.

She removed her hand from his lips, edged back. 'This really is a most irrational time of day.'

She was doing her best to keep things light. For both their sakes he had to play along. 'Disrupted sleep patterns can play havoc with a person's judgement.' And obviously their sanity. 'Sleep deprivation is a form of torture.'

'Believe me, at the moment so is my breath. It reeks! You've had a lucky escape, Luke Hillier. I best go and brush my teeth.'

He threw his head back and laughed. He had no idea how she could dispel the tension so easily, but he was grateful for it—another one of those things he could add to his list of good things to be grateful for. He helped her to her feet. 'Goodnight, Keira.'

'Goodnight, Luke.'

But after she left Luke couldn't help wishing they'd both been irrational for just a little bit longer.

He knew he'd really flay himself for that thought later.

For dinner the following evening Keira cooked steak and steamed new potatoes, and served them with a salad. As far as Luke was concerned it was as good as the previous night's lasagne.

Jason must have enjoyed it too, because, although subdued,

he ate everything placed in front of him. He even went back for a second serving of potatoes.

Luke followed suit and then, as casually as he could, asked, 'What do you have on for tomorrow? Any plans?'

Jason's fork, heaped with potato, halted halfway to his mouth. He stared at Luke as if he couldn't quite process the question. Luke's gut clenched. Had he cut himself off so completely from his son that a simple question could stupefy him?

Luke sliced a potato in two, although he no longer had the appetite to eat it. 'I really want that boundary paddock sown this autumn, but there's a lot of work to do before then. If you don't have any plans for tomorrow, and could see your way to giving me a hand, I'd be grateful.'

'Yeah? Sweet!' Jason's eyes lit up. But in the next instant he assumed that whole teenage nonchalant slouch again. 'I mean—yeah, no sweat.'

Luke tried to hide his grin. 'Thanks, son.' He tucked in to his potato with renewed enthusiasm.

After dinner Jason didn't immediately leap up from the table, so Luke pulled in a deep breath. 'I was rummaging through one of the sheds the other day, looking for a crowbar, and came across a couple of boxes your mum and I brought back from the city.'

'Some of Mum's things?' Jason stared at him. 'I thought Gran and Grandad had all her stuff.'

Luke rubbed a hand across his nape and forced himself to keep talking. 'This is stuff we bought together. Plus some books and photo albums.'

Jason leaned forward eagerly. 'Can I see? I—'

He broke off and eyed Luke warily, as if he expected Luke to holler no and storm from the room.

Luke had to swallow before he could speak. 'I thought that if you wanted to help me haul them out we could go through them. This place is looking a bit...dull.' All of Keira's colour had brought that home to him. 'From memory, we had some nice stuff.'

No matter how nice Tammy had made their apartment in the city, though, Luke had never stopped longing for home.

'When?' Jason had lost all pretence at nonchalance. 'Now?'

'As soon as we've helped Keira with the dishes.'

The grin she sent him when she turned from the sink made him feel a million dollars.

CHAPTER SIX

'You're baking?'

Keira swung around from taking the last sheet of cookies from the oven, to find Luke silhouetted in the kitchen doorway, bringing with him the scent of the outdoors and a reminder of her own wayward desires. Her hand shook. She hastily set the tray down on a rack to cool, and wiped suddenly damp palms down the sides of her shorts. 'I'm practising.'

'I like the sound of that.'

Backlit by the sun she sensed rather than saw his grin. He and Jason had spent yesterday working in the fields, and ever since Luke had seemed to find it a whole lot easier to smile. Which was great, she told herself, a definite improvement. Even if those smiles were proving lethal to her pulse.

It would be a bigger improvement if she could forget about kissing him. But all it took was one glimpse of those broad shoulders and strong thighs and yearning would stretch through her, pulling her skin thin and tight across her bones— as it had when they'd sat on the floor together at that ridiculous time the other morning.

Dwelling on that, though, wouldn't help. You're a strong, independent woman, she reminded herself.

She waved a hand at the cooling cookies and tried to banish all thoughts of broad shoulders, strong thighs and kissing from her mind. 'All the best mums bake.'

A chuckle emerged from the strong column of his throat.

Before her thoughts could go all wayward again she added, 'I just know I have a speciality.'

'Speciality?'

'You know—something that will make my kid swoon whenever he or she smells it baking or sees it cooling on the kitchen table.' She gestured to the cookies. 'Like choc-chip cookies or scones or pineapple upside-down cake or pikelets.'

'Or lamingtons or lemon-meringue pie,' he supplied, that grin still stretching through his voice.

'Exactly! So much baking, so little time. You can see why I have to start practising now.'

Christmas and cakes and birthday parties and bedtime stories—they were what childhood memories were made of. She might not be able to give her baby a father, but she was working on the baking and the bedtime stories. She'd bought a stack of children's books the other day in town, and when no one else was in the house she'd taken to reading them out loud. She wanted to get all those funny voices just right. Besides, her pregnancy books told her that her baby would hear her voice while it was in the womb, and would recognise it once it was born. The thought thrilled her.

She couldn't wait to hold her baby in her arms!

'Oh, Luke.' She clasped her hands beneath her chin and recalled what he'd said about the first moment Jason had been laid in his arms. Magic—that was how he'd described it. 'Wouldn't you just love to have another baby?'

'No!'

His vehemence startled her. The choc-chip cookie goodness leached from the air, the wholesome baking scents dissipating in the face of Luke's stark denial. Her mouth went dry. Did he hate single parenthood so much?

She tried to erase the frown from her face, moderate her shock. He and Jason had sorted everything out, hadn't they?

Everything between them was good again, wasn't it? So why…?

He dragged a hand down his face. 'I will never have more children.'

He said it with such quiet finality it made her blood run cold, and she wasn't even sure why. 'Why not?'

His lips twisted, but not a spark of humour lit his eyes. 'Let's just say that marriage and I are a poor pairing.'

There was nothing she could say in answer to that.

He pulled his hand away and shoved his shoulders back. 'Is that what you have planned for the rest of the afternoon?' He gestured towards the oven, the table. 'Baking?'

'Um, no. It seems silly to bake more than we could eat.' She tried to shake off the sombre cloud that threatened to descend over her. How this man chose to live his life, the decisions he made, was none of her business. 'Why?'

'I've finished my work in record time today, and I've just dropped Jason off at his grandparents'…'

'So?' She strove as hard as she could to be casual.

'I wondered if you'd like to take a drive down to the river? I was going to make some sandwiches, grab a nectarine or four and a couple of cans of soda, and head on down there.'

A picnic? His thoughtfulness suddenly touched her. He wanted to make sure she rested up and ate well, didn't he? 'That sounds lovely.' She held her arms out and turned on the spot. 'Will I be okay to go as I am?'

She wore navy cargo shorts and a raspberry singlet top. Luke's eyes darkened as they travelled over her, and her insides expanded while her skin contracted, making her hot and cold all at once.

He glanced away at the same moment she did. 'Do you have a long-sleeved shirt you could put on over that? You're very fair. You look as if you could burn up.'

Oh, she was burning up all right—but it had nothing to do with summer heat.

'You'll need to wear a hat, and slap on plenty of sun-screen too.'

With that he turned and pulled a loaf of bread towards him, his shoulders stiff with tension. She gritted her teeth and reminded herself that kissing him was a seriously bad idea. Why was it that all her common sense flew out of the window whenever she so much as glanced in Luke's direction?

'Friends,' she mumbled under her breath, retreating to her bedroom to find shoes and a shirt. 'Friends,' she intoned, slathering on sunscreen. 'Friends,' she whispered, standing in the hallway.

Pasting on a big smile, she breezed into the kitchen. 'Have you made those sandwiches yet, Hillier?' She *could* do friends.

'Packed and ready, Keely.'

He grinned, and predictably Keira's heart thump-thumped. She clapped her hands. 'Well, let's get this picnic on the road.'

'Hat?' he demanded.

'Oh um… I keep forgetting to buy one.'

He rolled his eyes. He dropped one on her head as she walked past. 'It's an old one of Jason's.'

She touched a hand to its brim and warmth billowed in her chest. *Friends,* she reminded herself.

'Oh, Luke,' Keira breathed as he pulled the ute to a halt by a stand of gums.

'Is this good enough for you, Keely?'

She heard the grin in his voice, but she didn't turn to grin back because somewhere between here and the homestead she'd come to the conclusion it would be a whole lot easier to do the friends thing if she kept her eyes firmly averted from broad shoulders and rich brown eyes.

Unfortunately she'd only gone on to notice how tanned and muscled his forearms were, how sure and strong his hands on the steering wheel. So she'd decided it might be best to avert her gaze from them too.

She hadn't worked out how to prevent his voice from doing that mush thing to her insides yet, though. She supposed she could always stop her ears with her fingers if she didn't care what he thought of her.

But she did care.

Dangerous, a little voice whispered through her.

She ignored it. She'd be leaving here in two days—how dangerous could one little picnic be? Besides, it had been interesting listening to him talk about the farm. He was working on improving the seventy hectares of pasture at the western end of the property. He was clearing weeds by hand because down the track he meant to go organic. It sounded exciting.

The enthusiasm in his voice had caught at her. She admired his dedication. Not to mention the view spread out before her now. *That* stole her breath.

'I… This is…' She couldn't find words to do it justice, so she pushed out of the car and made her way to the top of the bank to gaze down at the river below. Directly beneath her was a strip of sand that glittered gold, bound on either side by boulders and tall grass. The river flowed by smoothly, the water so clean and clear she could see the sand and pebbles in the shallows.

'The Namoi River,' Luke said from beside her.

In the field on the other side of the river something green grew. Its particular deep hue in combination with the shade provided by the trees behind her and all that gold…

'Canola,' he said, gesturing to the field opposite.

She spun to him. She couldn't help it. 'This place is gorgeous!'

'It is today.' He pushed the brim of his hat back. 'You should see it when there's been rain upriver in the ranges. The water roars through here like you wouldn't believe.'

He loved it then too, she could tell. She pointed to the strip of sand. 'Can we have our picnic down there?'

'That's the plan. Head on down while I grab the food.'

'Is it safe to paddle?'

'As safe as houses,' he promised, halfway back to the car already.

The second she hit the sand, she kicked off her sandals and plunged her feet into the water. It was cool and pleasant against her over-heated flesh. She wished Luke had told her to bring a swimsuit.

In the next instant she fanned her face. She and Luke with nothing on between them but thin Lycra and a pair of board shorts? *Not* a good idea.

'It gets colder further out,' Luke said, obviously mis-interpreting her face fanning. He settled himself on a rock. He didn't come any closer.

Keira rolled up her shorts a couple of extra inches and waded out up to her knees. 'It's lovely,' she called back.

He nodded and stayed exactly where he was. So she waded back to shore and sat on the sand nearby. Not too close.

She rested back on her hands and lifted her face to the sun. This was like being on holiday—heavenly—and she was determined to enjoy it while she could. 'C'mon, Hillier, pass out the sandwiches. I'm starving, and I'm eating for two, you know.'

With a low laugh, he tossed her a packet of sandwiches.

They munched them in silence, staring out at the river and taking deep breaths of gold-green goodness. When she glanced up, she found him watching her. 'What?'

'I wanted to thank you for the advice you gave me about Jason the other night. It's made a difference. An enormous difference.'

'So working together yesterday was good?'

He nodded. 'I can't believe how badly I let things slide with him.'

She wanted to tell him he'd had a lot on his mind—being thrust into the role of single parent, trying to work the farm single-handedly, dealing with Tammy's parents' bitterness— but she sensed he wasn't interested in making excuses.

'Have the two of you talked about Tammy?' She'd left him and Jason alone together on Tuesday night. She'd hoped that over those boxes they'd dragged in from the shed that Jason would find the courage to ask Luke the questions he needed to.

'Yeah.'

She grimaced for him. 'Hard?'

'Hell,' he bit out. Then frowned. 'It was hell at first,' he amended. 'It got easier as it went along.'

Her stomach unclenched.

'Tammy's parents have been telling Jason that mine and Tammy's separation is what caused her brain tumour.'

Tammy had died of a brain tumour? Oh, poor Tammy! Keira abandoned her sandwich.

'I told Jason that's not the truth.' His lips twisted. 'I know because I asked her doctor at the time.'

So he'd thought...

Her heart burned. She curled her hands into the sand. She ached to go to him to put her arms around him and offer whatever comfort she could. She suspected, though, that he wouldn't welcome her sympathy, so she stayed where she was.

'Is that why you and Tammy moved back here from the city?'

He shook his head. 'We moved back here six months before she was diagnosed.'

She cocked her head to one side. 'You know, I can't imagine you in the city.'

One corner of his mouth kicked up, but the smile didn't reach his eyes. 'It was Tammy's dream to live there. We moved not long after we were married.' He paused. 'It wasn't my cup of tea.'

She digested that silently. From the expression on his face, he'd loathed it. 'How long did you live there?'

'Nearly eleven years.'

She straightened and gaped at him. 'You...*you*...lived in the city for nearly eleven years?' To her he seemed as elemental as the gum trees up there on the bank. He seemed an extension of the landscape. Eleven years in the city. Wow! 'What did you *do* there?'

'I was apprenticed to a motor mechanic not long after we arrived. I like tinkering with engines, and it's a handy trade to have when you're living on the land.'

So even in the city he'd always had one eye trained on Candlebark?

His lips tightened. 'Moving to the city seemed the least I could do in the circumstances. As you can imagine, our parents were less than pleased when they found out we were expecting a baby. It felt good to get away. And Tammy and me...we were best friends from our first day in kindergarten. I pulled her plait and made her cry. She kicked my shin and made *me* cry.'

He looked suddenly young, as if this was one memory that couldn't hurt him. Keira smiled. 'Sounds like the basis of a lasting friendship to me.'

One corner of his mouth lifted. 'I can't remember a time when she wasn't a part of my life.' The smile faded. 'So I thought when we married... But I was wrong. We wanted different things from life.'

She wanted to tell him that these things happened, that he and Tammy had been too young, but the sudden darkness in his eyes kept her quiet.

'Dad was having some health issues, and we moved back so I could help him out for a bit. We rented a place in town. There was plenty of room at the homestead, but...'

'You wanted your own place,' she finished for him.

'I couldn't believe what bad shape Candlebark was in, and I knew Tammy would go stir crazy out here with me in the fields from sunrise to sunset. At least living in town she could visit her parents and friends.' He rubbed the back of his neck. 'She went stir crazy anyway. She wanted to return to the city almost immediately. I didn't. Our marriage only lasted another three months.'

'I'm sorry.'

He shrugged and stared down at his hands. 'Not long after that she was diagnosed with the tumour. She refused to let me move back in to help her.'

She glanced at him, and her heart burner harder and fiercer. 'Her parents blamed you for that?' she whispered.

'After she died they started all sorts of dreadful rumours. My parents couldn't bear the speculation whenever they went into town—the snubs and the looks—so they moved to the coast.'

And left Luke to cope on his own! No wonder he'd buried himself out here and thrown himself into farm work.

She had to swallow down a sudden lump. 'Have you told Jason what you just told me?'

'A lot of it.'

'And is he…?' What was the word Jason used? 'Sweet about it?'

He surveyed her for a long moment. 'It really matters to you, doesn't it?'

She shrugged a bit self-consciously. 'I guess it does. Crazy, huh? I've only known you guys for all of five minutes.'

He stared out at the river, lips pursed. 'It doesn't feel crazy,' he admitted.

'Must be all those irrational conversations we've been holding in the wee small hours,' she teased.

'That must be it.'

He grinned, and Keira suddenly remembered that the sun

was shining, it was nearly Christmas, and she was having a baby. And, from the look in Luke's eyes, the future looked bright for more than just her.

'Yeah, Jason and I are good. That's thanks in large part to you.'

'I didn't really do much.'

'You opened my eyes. I will always be *grateful* for that.'

She smiled at the emphasis. His approbation felt good—better than it had any right to—but she allowed herself the luxury of basking in it anyway. Because in two days she'd be leaving this place. In the long term she suspected this man could prove a challenge to all her carefully laid plans...not to mention her peace of mind. He could lay it all to waste. She also knew that two days was not enough time to create that kind of havoc inside her.

The thought of leaving, though, darkened her day for a moment. She shrugged it off. She had a wonderful future to look forward to. That was what she had to focus on.

'Have you sorted everything out with the house?'

Another shaft of sadness pierced her. 'I've signed the last of the paperwork and found myself another estate agent. My great-aunt's house will officially go on the market next week.'

'Congratulations.'

'Thank you.' She fought to find a smile. She should be smiling! She'd done what she'd come here to do. It was just... She didn't know why, but it somehow seemed wrong to sell her great-aunt's house.

'You don't seem all that happy about it.'

She should have known he'd sense her disquiet. 'I feel a bit guilty about selling it,' she confessed. 'Like I'm returning a gift someone has given me.'

'You know...' He pursed his lips. 'Something struck me when we inspected it the other day. With just a little bit of work your aunt's house would make the perfect home business.

You could extend out the back and convert the front into that clinic of yours.'

Keira's mind instantly shot off in a million different directions. 'Are you suggesting that I move here? That I set my clinic up in Gunnedah?'

He shrugged, and sent her the kind of grin that had her pulse tripping over itself. 'Why not?'

'But...I don't know anyone here.'

'You know me and Jason. It wouldn't take you long to make friends. Country towns have a community spirit I think you'd like. Believe me, you wouldn't lack for eager babysitters.' He stretched his legs out in front of him and gestured with one arm. 'And look at all this. It's a great place to grow up.'

He loved his home. That much she could tell. When he'd outlined his plans for the farm on their drive down here she'd started to see the place through his eyes. It had given her a whole new appreciation for it. 'But to move out here...' Her heart raced.

'Medical practitioners of all kinds are in demand in rural areas like this. It's hard to lure people from the city. You wouldn't have any trouble establishing yourself.'

'I...' She tried to shake herself out from under the spell he was weaving about her.

He sent her another one of those grins. 'It's just a thought. But it's worth thinking about, isn't it?'

'I...yes.' She drew the word out slowly. 'I guess it is.'

She'd have to sit down with a pen and a pad later, and work out the pros and cons. She sucked her bottom lip into her mouth. She could always rent out her flat in the city. That would provide her with a steady source of income and—

Later, she told herself firmly. This wasn't the kind of decision she could make on the spur of the moment. It needed careful consideration.

She glanced at Luke, and warmth curled in the pit of her stomach. She did her best to banish it. This wasn't the kind of decision where she'd allow her feelings for a man to sway her—no matter how broad his shoulders or devastating his smile. This came down to a straight business decision and whether this kind of life would be better for her and her Munchkin.

Still, it would be nice to have Luke as a friend.

'If need be, would you rent your room to me for another week some time in January?' Just in case this idea warranted further investigation.

'Of course.'

Excitement billowed through her—a sense of new possibilities opening up before her. She reached for a nectarine and bit into it. Juice promptly ran down her chin. She wiped it away with a laugh. 'Stone fruit is one of my favourite things about this time of year.'

'What are the others?'

'Christmas carols.' He rolled his eyes so she added, 'Not the jingly-jangly ones—though I quite like them too. I'm talking about the slow ones. You know—"Silent Night", "The First Noel", "The Little Drummer Boy"… They're beautiful songs, and they do what all good music should do.'

'Which is?'

'They make you feel…fuller.'

He didn't roll his eyes. He didn't say anything.

Keira bit into her nectarine again, tried to catch the juice that ran down her hand. She held the fruit away from her body. 'I'm going to need a bath after I've finished this.' Even so, she couldn't remember the last time she'd enjoyed a piece of fruit so much.

She went to take another bite, but made the mistake of glancing up at Luke first. His eyes had darkened, and he stared at her mouth with such fascination it made things inside her heat up then melt down. She gulped and tried to remember the friends thing. And that this was a *rational* time of day. Dear Lord, what had they been talking about?

Um… Uh… Christmas!

'You should really do something special for Jason for Christmas, you know. All kids need Christmas—even teenagers.' Instinct told her Luke needed it too. 'There's a magic to Christmas you can't get at any other time of year.' He didn't reply, so she stared doggedly out at the water. From the corner of her eye she could discern his gaze, hot and fierce on her face. If he didn't stop that soon she'd have to dive fully clothed into the river before she burned up.

She recognised the precise moment his gaze shifted to her legs. It was as if he'd reached out and stroked her with one lean, tanned finger. A quiver ran through her. Her breathing sped up. So did his. Her nerves drew tauter, tighter, until she thought they'd catapult her into something she'd regret.

It would be something Luke would definitely regret.

'Stop looking at me like that!'

She didn't want to be anybody's regret. Especially not at this time of the year. 'Tis the season and all that. She had a lot to be grateful for: that was what she wanted to focus her energies on. Not on a pair of firm lips and a strong, square jaw, or the way tawny eyes could darken to chocolate.

Luke leapt to his feet with a cut off imprecation. 'Why don't you wash in the river? I'll go grab a towel from the car.'

He stomped up the bank in the direction of the car. Keira fled to the river. Even if men weren't off her agenda, Luke was the last man she'd ever get involved with. He didn't want any more children, for a start.

With hands that shook, she did her best to wash the sticky remains of nectarine from her fingers and face. Because she couldn't stay in the river all day, and because she wanted to project an air of nonchalance for when Luke returned, she moved back to where they'd been sitting and propped herself against a rock. She started to unroll the legs of her shorts—

And froze.

A snake stared at her from the bottom of the track that Luke had just ascended. Its black eye—unlidded—didn't reflect the light. It lifted its head, and its forked tongue tasted the air.

Oh, help!

Keira stayed frozen. She might be a city girl, but she knew a brown snake when she saw one.

Brown snakes were bad.

Adrenaline shot through her in icy waves. Could the snake sense it? *The bad brown snake.* No—*no,* some logical part of her brain tried to reason. Snakes weren't bad. They were just one of Nature's vast array of creatures.

Yeah, and the venom from the bite of a brown snake could fell a grown man in—

'Keira?'

Luke's low tones. She could sense him at the top of the track.

'Keira, look at me.'

No way was she taking her eyes off that snake. If it made so much as the smallest move towards her, she was out of here.

'Keira, I can see the snake. Please…look at me.'

Something in his voice snagged at her. Almost against her will she lifted her gaze. He was too far away for her to pinpoint the exact shade of brown of his eyes, but she couldn't mistake the intensity in his face.

'Keira, you're doing great—you really are. I need you to keep doing more of the same.'

He wanted her to stay here?

'Any sudden movements will frighten it.'

She gulped.

'I'm not going to let anything bad happen to you, okay?'

She swallowed. 'Okay,' she mouthed back, because her vocal cords refused to work. The constriction around her lungs eased a fraction.

'You're between the snake and the river. He wants to go down for a drink.'

How did he know that? Had he and the snake exchanged

pleasantries as they'd passed on the path? She couldn't help it. She slipped a hand over her abdomen.

His eyes narrowed. 'I am not going to let anything bad happen to your baby either!'

He spoke so fiercely tears stung her eyes—those darn pregnancy hormones—but she believed him. He was like some old-fashioned hero from a book or a movie. He knew how to take care of his own.

Not that she was *his*, of course.

But she did trust him—with her life. And her baby's.

'In a moment I'm going to start drumming the ground with my feet. The snake will want to avoid something that sounds as big as me, so it's going to shoot off down to the river and probably all the way across it.'

It was going to slither right by her?

'I want you to stay as still as a statue.'

She pulled in a breath. Finally she nodded. When Luke looked at her like that she had a feeling she could do just about anything. She closed her eyes. It would be easier to focus on staying still if she didn't catch sight of that snake again.

She heard Luke's thumping—she would have had to be deaf not to. She didn't hear the snake at all. She tried to empty her mind of all thought and concentrate on keeping her body as still as possible.

'Keira?'

Her name was a mere whisper on the air, and so close she had to open her eyes. Were they safe? Had the snake gone away? Had Luke been bitten?

Before she could utter a single one of her questions Luke scooped her up in his arms and strode up the bank towards the car. She couldn't help it. She started shaking as if she were cold and couldn't get warm. All that pent up adrenaline, some rational part of her reasoned.

'Did you get bitten?' she finally managed to get out from between chattering teeth

'No.'

'Me neither,' she said, which was a ridiculous thing to say, because he'd have seen it if the snake had struck her.

Luke opened the passenger door and slid onto the seat with her on his lap. She continued to shake. 'Sorry,' she mumbled, 'I can't seem to help it. What a wimp, huh?'

His arms tightened about her. 'You weren't a wimp. You were wonderfully brave.'

Keira closed her eyes and gave herself up to the comfort of being in his arms. She rested her cheek against his shoulder and drew in all the strength and reassurance she needed.

Luke's heartbeat didn't slow until Keira's shaking started to ease. He found he still couldn't loosen his arms from around her yet.

He bit back something rude and succinct. When he'd first seen that snake, and registered the fear on Keira's face, an anger so fierce and scalding had gripped him it had almost left no room for reason.

He'd remembered himself just in time.

Tell me three things you're grateful for.

Keira was alive and safe in his arms. He was grateful for that.

Snakes might be a protected species in Australia, but if it had bitten her he'd have torn it apart with his bare hands.

She adjusted herself in his arms, sat up a little. He reluctantly loosened his hold, but didn't let her go.

He'd let her go in a moment, he told himself. When he was one hundred percent sure she was okay.

Her eyes met his. 'Thank you for rescuing me.' Her hand inched across her stomach. 'For rescuing us. I didn't have a clue what to do.'

'You did great.' She had too. She'd wanted to run, he'd read that in her face, but she'd conquered her fear and followed his instructions.

Tell me three things you're grateful for.

He was grateful she hadn't been bitten.

She gestured to herself in his lap. 'What a big baby you must think me.'

He didn't think her a baby. Not at all. She was feminine and soft and, for all her slightness, curvy where it counted. Which was an unfortunate thought to have when she was in his arms like this. Very unfortunate. And bewitching.

'I think you're brave and lovely.' Perhaps he shouldn't have said that last bit.

Dammit, though, she *was* lovely!

With a smile, she reached up and brushed her lips across his cheek in the lightest of kisses. He felt its impact all the way down to the soles of his feet.

'Thank you,' she whispered.

The scent of vanilla engulfed him, and something inside him melted. He stared into her grey eyes—her beautiful grey eyes—then he leant forward and placed his lips on hers.

She didn't close her eyes. He didn't close his. He moved his lips over hers—gentle, testing, ready to draw back at the slightest hint or hesitation from her—but after a moment of stunned stillness her lips softened and shaped themselves to his.

And then her eyelids fluttered closed.

With a groan, Luke gathered her closer. She tasted so good. She tasted so...*good*!

He ran his tongue across her bottom lip. She gasped and trembled. That gasp reached right inside his chest and dragged him under. Her hand dived into the hair at his nape to pull him closer. Her lips opened under his and he lost himself in the taste, the sensation...the freedom of kissing Keira.

The taste of her, the feel of her, woke parts of him that had been dead and numb for too long. Her hand burrowed its way beneath his shirt to trace the contours of his chest. He thought his lungs might burst with need when she ran the palm of her hand back and forth across his nipple.

With one arm anchoring her to him firmly, he traced her body from hip to breast. Slowly. He cupped and teased her through the cotton of her singlet top until she writhed and arched against him.

'Oh, Luke...please,' she begged, her moans and his ragged breathing filling the interior of the car.

He knew what she meant. He'd never wanted a woman with such a savage need before.

With something midway between a groan and a growl, he swept his hand down to her hip and across her stomach to the waistband of her shorts. He wanted to touch every part of her. He wanted to kiss every inch of her. His fingers brushed across her stomach again, and something tugged at his consciousness.

Keira.

Pregnant.

Baby.

He stilled. He knew enough to know that making love would not harm her baby, but the reality brought him up short.

He met the clear grey eyes surveying him. He swallowed, then forced words out of uncooperative lips. 'I can't offer you anything more than this.' His voice came out hoarse, as if he needed a drink.

He couldn't offer this lovely woman any of the things she deserved. All he could give her was momentary pleasure...a brief affair.

He watched her consider the idea. If he were an honourable man he'd let her go, but he couldn't. God help them both if she reached up and kissed him now—gave him her tacit agreement—because he would not have the strength to hold back.

Even though she deserved so much more.

He dragged a hand down his face. When he pulled it away, he saw her answer framed in the regret that stretched through her eyes.

Be grateful for what you do have.

Grinding back a torrent of expletives, he slid her off his lap and all but fell out of the car. He closed the door before he could change his mind. He took a moment to straighten his clothes, gather himself. Gave her the time to do the same, before walking around to the driver's side and sliding in behind the steering wheel.

Be grateful for what you do have.

It didn't matter which way he looked at it—he couldn't be grateful for this. Leaving the warmth of Keira's arms was the hardest thing he'd ever had to do.

CHAPTER SEVEN

LUKE found himself whistling as he strode towards the homestead. The light was fading from the sky and a satisfying weariness was settling over his limbs. In another hour it would be completely dark. In less than fifteen minutes he, Jason and Keira would be seated around the kitchen table, enjoying another of her superb meals.

It was her last night—on this visit at least, he knew she'd be back—and he couldn't wait to see what she served for dinner. He moved with an eager step across the veranda, pushed open the door...and immediately sensed something was wrong.

A roast chicken and vegetables squatted promisingly in the oven, but the oven itself had been turned off. A saucepan of peas and another of gravy sat on top of the stove, but the hotplates had been switched off too. The table was only half laid.

He touched a hand to the side of one of the saucepans—still warm. Keira's morning sickness must have struck again.

He headed for the bathroom.

He hesitated for only a moment before tapping on the door. 'Keira, is everything okay?'

No answer.

He tried the door. Locked. He tapped louder. 'Keira?'

From behind the door he heard a muffled movement, then the lock slid back and the door cracked open a fraction. Keira's pale, pinched face appeared, and fear clutched Luke's heart. He tried to rein in his panic, to keep his voice steady. 'Sweetheart, what's wrong?'

Her chin wobbled. She pressed her lips tight together for a moment, as if trying to get herself under control. Luke gripped the doorframe until the wood bit into his fingers.

She swallowed. 'Would you…would you be able to drive me to the hospital please?'

Her voice came out dull, weak. The sparkle had gone from her eyes.

Very gently, Luke pushed the door open. She didn't resist. He hooked an arm beneath her knees and lifted her, strode into the living room and laid her carefully on the sofa, placed cushions behind her knees to raise her legs. She didn't resist.

Jason leapt up. 'What's—?'

Luke silenced him with a look. Seizing the phone, he called for an ambulance, and then moved back to Keira's side to take her hand. It lay in his unmoving, so small and defenceless… so limp. 'They'll be here soon,' he told her.

She closed her eyes, but he'd read the expression in them.

Her fingers were so cold! He wanted to kiss them warm. A lump thickened his throat. He wrapped her hand in both his own and held on tight.

CHAPTER EIGHT

'I'M SORRY, Luke, but your friend has had a miscarriage.'

Luke stared at the doctor—a man he'd known his entire life—and tried to make sense of the words that left the older man's lips.

'I'm sorry.'

The doctor's sympathy hit him with the force of a combine harvester at full tilt. He couldn't speak for a moment. *Keira had lost her baby.*

'You're sure?'

The question didn't deserve an answer—Dr Metcalfe had been a member of the medical profession for nearly forty years—but he nodded and squeezed Luke's shoulder.

She'd lost her baby!

'I need to see her.' He'd search every room in the hospital if he had to.

'You can take her home.'

That pulled him up short. 'I...don't you have to make sure she's okay? Make her well again?' He didn't care that it was nearly Christmas and staff were on leave. This was Keira they were talking about. He would not stand for inferior medical care or—

'Luke, Keira's not sick. She doesn't have any kind of infection or disease we can treat. She's had a miscarriage. She wasn't that far along in her pregnancy, and there's very little bleeding. She might be a little tender for a few days, but there's nothing more we can do for her.'

'What caused it?' he burst out. He should have kept a closer eye on her, made her rest more.

'Sometimes it just…happens.'

Luke's shoulders slumped. Keira had lost her baby. He wanted to find her, pull her into his arms and comfort her.

He had a feeling she wouldn't let him. Or, worse still, she'd submit because she knew it was too late and it didn't matter any more. Like she had when he'd carried her from the bathroom to the sofa. She'd known then.

'Did she tell you she was undergoing IVF treatment?' He wasn't leaving until he was one hundred percent sure Dr Metcalfe had all the facts.

'Yes. I've sent a fax through to her doctor in Sydney.'

Luke closed his eyes. There was nothing…*nothing* he could do to reverse this.

The doctor led him through to the next room and pointed towards a cubicle. Luke swallowed, and then edged forward to peer around the curtain. Keira sat huddled in a chair, small and defenceless. His scowl fled. He wanted to reach out. He had to clench his hands to stop himself. This was about her and what she needed, not him.

He moved to the chair beside her. 'Keira?'

He winced at the dullness in her eyes, the grey pallor of her skin…her lack of vitality. When he reached out to touch her cheek she jerked away. Things inside him stretched tight. He wanted to howl for her. He beat the impulse down. 'Keira, I'm sorry.' He didn't add anything more. What else was there to say? Adding the other words *that you lost your baby* just seemed cruel.

And she looked exhausted.

She gave a curt nod. 'Thank you.' Perfunctory, as if he was a stranger. It stung.

'Are you ready to go home?'

'Yes, thank you.'

Luke sat by Keira's bedside all night.

She'd told him it wasn't necessary. He did it anyway. He wanted to be close by in case she needed something—a glass of water, another blanket…him. Her answer had been to pull the covers up to her neck and turn her face to the wall.

He'd switched off the lamp, but neither one of them had slept.

When the first fingers of dawn crept across the room, she slid out from beneath the covers.

Luke jerked in the chair. 'Where…?'

'Bathroom.'

He pulled in a breath. She seemed veiled behind a haze of nothingness. No colour, no bounce—nothing. And, although there was nothing wrong with her posture or with the way she walked, it seemed to him that she limped from the room—as if some essential component of her energy had been taken from her.

He dropped his head to his hands. He didn't know how to help her. And he wanted to help her. He forced himself to his feet and went to make coffee.

Keira was relieved to find Luke gone when she returned to her bedroom. She crawled back into bed, pulled the covers up to her chin. The effort of rising, of moving, had left her exhausted, and the dim grey of the dawn light filtering beneath the curtains suited her mood perfectly.

She clocked the exact moment Luke returned. He didn't say anything for a long moment. She didn't care. She welcomed the silence. Finally, 'Would you like coffee or toast?'

'No, thank you. I'll rest. Doctor's orders.' She didn't turn from staring at the wall. 'Go tend your farm, Luke. I'm not in the mood for company.'

He still hovered, but she refused to look at him. 'Promise you'll call if you need anything?'

It took a superhuman effort, but she managed to squeeze the words from between dry lips. 'I promise.' Anything to make him go away. She wouldn't need anything. She'd lost the only thing she needed. She just wanted to stare at the greyness of the wall and not move…not think…not feel.

Every movement she made only rendered her more aware of the hole that gaped through her, of the emptiness inside her. If she stayed very still, barely blinking, she might succeed in ignoring that emptiness, in preventing it from swallowing her whole.

Maybe.

Luke came back at lunchtime, but she feigned sleep and he went away again.

He came back mid-afternoon. She feigned sleep again, but this time he reached down and touched her shoulder. 'Keira?'

'Hmm?'

'You have to eat something.'

'I'm not hungry.' The thought of food made her feel sick. Not literally sick—not nausea sick—not morning sickness sick. Only yesterday—

She cut the thought dead.

To eat she'd have to move. Moving would remind her of what she'd had yesterday. And what she didn't have today. 'I'm not hungry,' she repeated.

'Keira, if you won't eat at least one piece of toast and drink a glass of orange juice I'm going to take you back to the hospital and have them readmit you.'

He kept his voice low and quiet. For that much she was grateful. She thought about the hospital—all those rattling trolleys and cheerful nurses. She forced herself into a sitting position and took the plate and glass he held out to her. She froze when he reached out a hand, as if he meant to push her hair back from her face.

He dropped it back to his side and sank into that chair again. Keira didn't look at him. She knew what she'd see in his face, and she didn't think she could bear it.

She ate the toast and drank the juice. She handed the plate and glass back to him. She didn't say thank you. She wasn't thankful. He left a bottle of water on her bedside table. She knew in his place she'd do the same. He didn't deserve her irritation, her ingratitude.

She lay back down and stared at the wall. She didn't have the energy for irritation.

When he returned later that evening, with a steaming mug of cocoa made with full-cream milk, she sat up without a word and drank it.

The food and the drink didn't make her feel better. It didn't make her feel worse either.

And at some stage during the night she even managed some sleep.

When Luke tapped on her door the next morning and entered, Keira forced herself up into a sitting position. But Luke didn't hand her a plate of toast or a glass of juice. She glanced up.

'I'm sorry, Keira, you're going to have to get up.'

He spoke briskly. It made her blink. Resentment churned through her at this invasion into her sanctuary. 'Why?'

'Because I need to clean your room.'

Her jaw dropped. 'No, you don't!'

'Yes, I do. This room gets a thorough clean once a week.' His shoulders lifted. 'As you pointed out, Candlebark has few enough attractions, but at least the cleanliness of the room is one of the things a prospective tenant can count on.'

She stared at him and tried to work out what he was talking about. She pressed her fingers to her temples. 'What day is it?'

She counted back. 'It's Sunday, isn't it? I was suppose to leave yesterday.'

She scrambled out of bed. She'd been so caught up in her own stuff she hadn't stopped to think what a burden she'd become to Luke. He didn't deserve that. He had a farm to run, a paddock to clear, wheat to harvest. While all she could do was lie in bed and make a nuisance of herself.

'I'll pack and be out of your hair in under an hour. I promise.'

Luke caught her shoulders in his hands and turned her to face him. 'No.'

'What do you mean, no?' He must be dying to see the back of her. She didn't want to notice his steady gaze or the strength of his jaw, but she couldn't help it. She envied him them both.

'What I mean is that Jason and I would like you to stay on for a bit longer…and your room needs cleaning.'

'But…why?' She couldn't think of any conceivable reason why they would want her to stay—not in her current state— unless… 'Are you feeling sorry for me?' She couldn't stand that thought. It filled her with dread. It made the darkness looming at the edge of her consciousness nudge closer.

'We are both truly sorry about your miscarriage, Keira.'

She flinched and pulled out of his grip, turned back towards the bed. No matter how much she wanted to, she couldn't crawl back beneath those covers. She pushed her shoulders back. She came from a long line of strong women. She would not be a burden to a virtual stranger.

'But that's not why we want you to stay. We've come to think of you as our friend.'

Oh! She turned.

Luke had his hands on his hips. He looked big and broad, and his size dominated the space. This might be a double-sized room, but when Luke entered it seemed to shrink.

'I know the doctor said that physically you're fine. I even

rang him this morning to make sure you'd be okay to drive home if that's what you want to do.'

He had? She tried to brace herself against the warmth threatening to steal over her at his thoughtfulness.

'He said it shouldn't be a problem. But...' Luke frowned. 'Think about it, Keira. Do you really want to return to the hustle and bustle of the city at Christmastime?'

She didn't even have to think about it. The unequivocal *no* slammed into her before Luke had finished the sentence.

'If you stay at Candlebark you can have all the peace and quiet you want.'

She had to admit it sounded tempting—a mini-haven before returning to the city and facing all her friends with her un-happy tidings. She wished now she hadn't spread the news of her pregnancy so far and wide. She bit her lip. She wasn't due back at work for another two weeks...

Luke shifted his weight to the balls of his feet, as if ready-ing himself for a fight. He'd argue with her to stay in that no nonsense way of his because he thought it was what was best for her, in the same way he'd tackled her morning sickness with his cures.

But she no longer had morning sickness.

Unbidden, a whimper left her. Luke was at her side in seconds, easing her down to sit on the edge of the bed. 'Oh, Luke. I lost my baby.'

He pressed one of her hands between both his own. 'I know, sweetheart. I'm sorry.'

'I...' She swallowed. 'I can't face going back to the city and telling all my friends yet.'

'You don't have to. Stay here.'

The pressure of his hands reassured her. She searched his face. 'That sounds...nice. I'll pay for my room of course.'

'No, you won't. Last week you stayed as my lodger. This week I'm asking you to stay as my guest.'

One glance at his face told her she wouldn't change his mind. 'Then at least let me clean the room.'

'You sure you're up to it?'

'Positive.' It might be a blessing to have something to do.

'Then you have yourself a deal.'

Luke found Jason in the barn, rubbing down Dusty, his horse. He turned the moment Luke's boots scraped against the packed dirt floor.

'How's Keira?'

Luke shrugged, not quite sure how to answer. 'Do you mind if she stays on for a few more days?'

Jason's eyes widened at the question, and it suddenly occurred to Luke that he'd spoken on Jason's behalf earlier without a second thought. In fact he'd never once bothered to ask Jason how he felt about Luke renting out their spare room. Not once.

How much else had he taken for granted?

He set his shoulders. '*Do* you mind? I mean, it's your home too.'

'It'd be sweet if she stayed a bit longer.'

Luke nodded, and collapsed onto a bale of hay. He was glad Keira had agreed to stay. It meant he could keep an eye on her, make sure she didn't neglect herself and become ill. Or, alternatively, didn't overdo things and make herself sick. He ached to do more. Her lack of colour, her lack of vibrancy, her utter lack of life, hurt him in a way he couldn't put into words. He wanted to find a way to put just a bit of that sparkle back into her eyes.

He started when Jason threw himself down on the hay bale beside him. 'You worried about her?'

'Just trying to think of something that might cheer her up.' He glanced at his son from the corner of his eye. 'Any suggestions?'

Jason scuffed the toe of one boot against the floor.

'Flowers?' In the next instant he shook his head. 'Nah, they won't help.'

They were both quiet for a while. 'That night at dinner,' Jason finally said, 'she said she liked Christmas.'

Luke lifted his head. 'She told me she loves Christmas carols.'

'Maybe we could buy of CD of carols and play it every day. And we could Christmas the house up a bit.'

Luke remembered what Keira had said to him the day of their picnic—that all kids needed Christmas, even teenagers, and that he should do something special for Jason.

'It's worth a shot, isn't it?' Jason added. 'We could try and talk her into staying for Christmas—that's only next Saturday—and we could have a nice dinner or something. I...I think she'd like that.'

Luke leapt to his feet. 'I think it's a brilliant idea.'

Jason grinned. 'Sweet.'

That grin tugged at Luke. He thought of all Keira had just lost, and how much he himself had and yet hadn't appreciated. 'You like her, don't you?'

Jason shrugged. 'She laughs a lot.'

And most of the adults in Jason's life didn't laugh—at least not much, Luke realised.

'And she likes people, and that makes it easy to like her. She doesn't brush you off because she's busy with her own stuff or anything.'

Not like him, Luke realised. He hadn't always been like that, though.

Jason moved back towards Dusty's stall. 'She's cool. She told me I should talk to you about Mum, and she was right.'

Luke blinked, but when he thought about it he realised it shouldn't have surprised him. 'She told me I should talk to you too. And she was right.'

Luke glanced down at his hands. 'Jason, your mum—she was a great mum, right?'

Jason nodded.

'She would've known what to do, known what you needed, if our positions had been reversed and she was here and I wasn't. I'm not so good at working that stuff out. I thought if I excused you from the farm chores and gave you plenty of spare time to hang out with your friends and your Gran and Grandad, and didn't remind you about your mum, that'd make things a bit easier for you. But I was wrong. I'm sorry.'

'Not sure I'm so good at it either,' Jason said, his voice gruff. 'And, yeah, Mum was a great mum, and I miss her loads and all, but I like living here better than the city.'

Luke let out a breath. 'So...we're sweet?'

'We're sweet.'

'Good.' With that, Luke started for the door.

'Dad?'

He swung back.

'Mum's not the only one who was good. You're a great dad too, you know?'

A lump formed in Luke's throat.

'And...I...uh...love you.'

Luke walked back and did something he hadn't done in a very long time. He pulled Jason into a rough hug. Jason hugged him back. Hard.

Luke did his best to swallow the lump. 'Thanks, son. I love you too.'

Keira dressed. And then she cleaned her room from top to bottom.

It didn't make her feel any worse. It didn't make her feel any better either. Eventually, though, she had to admit there was nothing left to clean in the room. If she didn't want to become a burden to Luke she had to stop hiding out in here. She glanced at her watch. It would be lunchtime soon. She could put the kettle on.

She forced unwilling legs out into the hallway and down its length to the main living area of the house. A part of her was grateful Luke wasn't in either the kitchen or the living room. The thought of making small talk had the strength draining from her arms and legs. Besides, she wanted him working those fields of his, not worrying about her.

She filled the kettle and switched it on. Drummed her fingers while she waited for it to boil and then reached for the teabags...and froze. Her mouth dried. A packet of liquorice tea sat innocuously on the counter beside all her other teas. The liquorice tea she wouldn't need again. She swung away, pulled out a chair at the kitchen table and sat.

Don't think about it!

The bright cover of a magazine drew her gaze. She reached out and tugged it towards her, desperate for the distraction. And froze again. Her pregnancy magazine! With its cover picture of a smiling baby—a chubby-cheeked baby dressed in cheerful red and...and smiling.

She slammed it face down, but that didn't help. A very pregnant woman graced the back cover, advertising a brand of stroller. Keira shoved her chair back and raced blindly into the living room, trying to block the images of that smiling baby and that pregnant woman from her mind.

She eased herself down to the sofa and closed her eyes, tried to focus on her breathing. When she opened them again they zeroed in on the tiny baby booties she'd left on the coffee table.

She couldn't move. All she could do was stare.

She'd left those booties there because she hadn't wanted to pack them away. She'd wanted to touch them, play with them...imagine the tiny feet that would wear them.

'Oh, Munchkin...'

Very slowly she reached out and gathered them in one hand. They were so very little. She lifted them and inhaled their clean woollen scent. They felt soft and warm against her face.

* * *

'Keira?'

Keira started. She didn't know how long she'd been sitting there with the booties pressed against her cheek. She pulled her hands and the booties down into her lap.

Luke moved into the room with that easy grace of his. He settled himself on the coffee table so they sat almost knee to knee. His heat and his breadth reached out to her in silent invitation. She knew all she had to do was lean across and he'd enfold her in his arms. It wouldn't make up for what had happened, for what she had lost, but she suspected it would help. She suspected that being held in his arms would make her feel safe for a bit.

But that would only be an illusion. She stiffened her spine and resisted the temptation.

'You okay?'

She didn't know if she'd ever be okay again, but she couldn't say that out loud because it would be a pathetic thing to say. Her mother would never have said it.

'I...' She pressed the booties between both hands. 'Trying to ignore what's happened isn't working.'

His eyes softened. 'Is that what you've been trying to do?'

She nodded. 'But I was just about to make a cuppa when I saw my liquorice tea sitting there, which reminded me of morning sickness and being...'

He nodded. She was grateful he didn't finish the sentence for her.

'And my pregnancy magazine was on the table, and it has the most gorgeous baby on the front cover and the most pregnantest woman on the back.' She didn't know if there was such a word, but she knew Luke would understand what she meant. 'And then when I came in here and found these...' She stopped worrying at the booties and held them up.

He dragged a hand down his face. 'I can't believe I didn't think to clear all that away.'

'It's not your fault.' He'd been too worried about whether she was eating enough, and if she was ever going to emerge from his spare bedroom or not.

She stared down at the booties and that darkness stretched through her. She curled her hand into a fist, crushing the delicate wool between her fingers. 'I'm trying to think what I could've done differently. Did I lift something too heavy? Have I been pushing myself too hard? Did I eat something I shouldn't have? Maybe that six-hour drive from Sydney—'

Luke reached out and closed his hands over hers, bringing a halt to her rush of words. 'You did everything you could to keep you and your baby healthy and safe, Keira. You didn't do anything wrong.'

'But...' That couldn't be true. If there was nothing she could do differently next time then...then there'd never *be* a next time.

'Dr Metcalfe said sometimes these things just happen for *no* conceivable reason.'

Then... She swallowed. She couldn't go through this again—not on her own. So much for priding herself on her independence!

She leapt to her feet, shoved the booties at Luke and started to pace. For as long as he sat so close the temptation to seek comfort in his arms beat at her—more proof of her weakness. 'I've let my mother and grandmother down!'

He shot to his feet. 'What on earth—?'

'They were both strong women who could do it all alone, but I'm not like that. I—'

'Garbage!'

His bluntness made her blink.

'Your mother didn't do it on her own. She might not have had your father around, but from what you've told me your grandmother was there for her every step of the way.'

Keira stared at him.

'I'm not denying that they were both strong women, but,

Keira, you're even stronger. You've shown more courage, not less. With eyes wide open you chose to have a baby without the usual support networks. That's amazing!'

But look where it had landed her!

'One day you will make a wonderful mother.'

No, she wouldn't. She didn't have what it took to travel down that path again. Not on her own.

'And it's not shameful to need other people, to rely on them. It's natural. You needed your mother and your grandmother, didn't you? People need other people—you taught me that. I need Jason. And I know I need to broaden my social network.' His lips twisted. 'I'm hoping it'll keep me more...balanced in future.'

His admission brought her up short. Had her idea of independence become skewed, affecting her judgement? Had she deliberately kept people—men—at a distance just to prove she could do it all on her own?

'Keira, you have your mother on an impossibly high pedestal.' He paused. 'Did she ever marry?'

She shook her head. 'Have you ever considered that what you took for independence was actually fear? After your father, maybe your mother was just too scared to trust a man again.'

Her voice shook. 'That's rich, coming from you.' All the same, her mind whirled.

'I'm not criticising your mother, Keira, but she was flesh and blood like the rest of us. And, like the rest of us, she must've made her fair share of mistakes.'

Her mother hadn't been perfect, of course, but...

Luke reached out and pushed a strand of hair behind her ear. 'She'd have *loved* the woman you've become, Keira. She'd have been proud of you.'

Keira's hands started to shake. And her knees. She crossed back over to the sofa and hunched up in one of its corners, arms tightly crossed to try and contain the shaking. 'I wish she were here now.'

Luke sat beside her. 'I wish she was too. I wish she could help you through this. Instead...' those firms lips of his twisted again '...you're stuck with me.'

He wanted to help her. She could see that. Somewhere in the last seven or eight days he really had come to see her as a friend.

'Is there anything I can do to make things easier?'

'Believe me, Luke, if I could think of a single thing that would make me feel better I'd...' Her voice trailed off.

His eyes narrowed. 'What?'

That gaping darkness loomed over her. She pushed it back with all her might and deliberately un-hunched her body. 'Brooding will send me mad! Is there something useful I can do? I don't know how good I'd be at digging out weeds, but I'd be willing to give it a go.'

She needed something to keep that yawning emptiness at bay. She swallowed. Deep down she knew it wasn't oblivion that lay at the heart of that darkness. It hid a swirling pit of pain and grief, and if she fell into it she didn't know how she'd ever get out again.

'I don't think that kind of physical work would be good for you at the moment,' Luke started slowly, 'but...'

She leant towards him eagerly. 'But?'

He raked a hand through his hair and grimaced. 'I'm not sure I should ask it of you.'

'Ask away,' she ordered, the swirling darkness retreating further with every passing second.

'It might seem...insensitive.'

That gave her pause, but only for a moment. 'Out with it.'

'You...um...told me that...'

His reluctance to continue started to irk her. Out of all proportion, she suspected. She gritted her teeth, clenched her hands, but the anger surging through her had become difficult to contain. 'Fine,' she snapped, shooting to her feet. 'I thought you wanted to help, but—'

'Whoa!' Luke grabbed her arm before she could flounce off. 'Christmas,' he said, before she could tug free or yell some more. 'You said I should do something for Jason for Christmas, but...what?'

The puzzle pieces fell into place. Carefully she detached her arm from his warm grip and sat again. 'I see. And you thought asking me to help might be insensitive because I might not feel much like celebrating Christmas after...after what's happened?'

He nodded.

'And I...' She moistened suddenly dry lips. 'I just went and snapped your head off.' What had got into her? 'I'm sorry.'

'Don't give it another thought. If I've asked too much, then just say.'

'No,' she said slowly, thinking of Jason and how his face had grown wistful when she'd described her Christmas plans to him. 'We don't have to go over the top, do we?'

Luke collapsed back down beside her, his shoulders slumping. 'Don't ask me. Christmas was never a big deal when I was growing up. Mum and Dad weren't really into it.'

Her heart contracted. They should have made a bigger effort for him.

'And it was Tammy who took care of all of that stuff when we were married.'

And since her death Luke and Jason hadn't had Christmas. The thought made her forget her own misery for a moment.

He frowned. 'From memory, though, it always cost a bomb.'

'It doesn't have to. A few decorations, a nice meal...a couple of small gifts.'

'Yeah? And Jason... He'd like that, you think?'

'He'll love it,' she assured him.

He stared at her for a moment. 'You really think you can bring Christmas to Candlebark?'

With her background, nothing could be easier. She nodded solemnly. 'I believe I can.'

His brow suddenly cleared. 'So you'll stay for Christmas?'

She found she could even smile. 'Yes.'

CHAPTER NINE

KEIRA glanced up from the kitchen table when Luke strode in early the following afternoon. He grabbed a bottle of water from the fridge and drank deeply. She tried not to notice the rippling muscles in his arms, or how strong and tanned he looked.

He gestured. 'You want one?' When she shook her head he closed the fridge door. 'What are you doing?'

'Deciding on the menu for our Christmas dinner.'

Interest sparked his eyes. 'Yeah?'

It almost made her smile, this latent excitement of his. She couldn't begin to thank him for the task he'd assigned her. It had helped take her mind off...other things. Whenever the darkness threatened, she threw herself into planning and list-making till it receded again. Simple.

He leant back against the kitchen cupboards. 'What have you decided—a seafood buffet?'

She shook her head. No way. Luke and Jason needed a proper traditional Christmas this year. To make up for the last three Christmases. 'We're having roast turkey with cranberry sauce, roast vegetables and Brussels sprouts.'

Luke frowned.

She bit her lip. 'You hate turkey?' They could have pork or chicken instead.

'It just sounds like a lot of hard work. I want you to be able to relax on the day too.'

'You needn't worry about that. You and Jason will be on vegetable peeling duty.' She wanted him to see how easy it all was so he could do it again next year.

'That's okay, then.'

'We've left it too late to make a Christmas pudding, so dessert will have to be either trifle or pavlova. We can vote on that at dinner tonight.'

'Sounds as if it's all coming together.'

'It is.'

'Good.' He took another long pull on his water. 'Are you busy this afternoon?'

Her ears pricked up. Did he have another task for her? Busy was good! She set her pen down. 'No.'

'Then I thought if you were interested we might go through your great-aunt's house one more time.'

Her stomach contracted.

'I wanted to show you what I meant about converting the place into that clinic of yours.'

But… Her hands snaked around her waist. That dream… it was dust now, and—

'You said you'd always planned to open your own clinic one day. There's absolutely nothing to stop you from going ahead with that plan.'

Her arms loosened. She sat back and considered his words. He was right, of course. There was nothing to prevent her from setting up her own physiotherapy practice in Gunnedah. If that was what she wanted to do.

She'd started to grow fond of the town. Whenever she popped in to do some shopping people smiled at her and made eye contact. Shop assistants and checkout operators always had time for a chat and a laugh. She pursed her lips. The relaxed pace suited her.

Plus, the countryside was pretty. That was an added attraction. Whenever she looked at that view of Luke's she had to smile, remembering the pride in his eyes and his complete

incomprehension that anybody could possibly find it wanting. Frankly, she was starting to come round to his way of
thinking.

And she *had* asked him to assign her a project. Turning
her great-aunt's house into her dream clinic fitted the bill
perfectly. After all, Christmas would only take her up till
Saturday.

'Okay.' She leapt to her feet.

He planted his hands on his hips and surveyed her through
narrowed eyes. 'You're sure?'

'You bet.'

Busy was good.

'This is what I was thinking…'

Keira followed Luke through the front door of her great-
aunt's house and then into the large reception room on the
left.

'This front room here would be your reception area.'

She turned on the spot and nodded. 'A desk there, with
some filing cabinets behind.' She pointed. 'Over there would
be the waiting area—a few chairs and a small coffee table for
magazines.'

'It's a large room, so you'd fit all that in no problems.'

He was right.

'A bonus is this big front window overlooking the park. If
for some reason mums or dads have to bring their school-age
children with them, the kids could play in the park and their
parents would still be able to keep an eye on them from in
here.'

Keira could feel herself start to hunch at the mention of
children.

'You could even put a couple of chairs on the veranda with
that in mind.'

'Right.' She nodded. 'Good idea.' Her voice came out
strained and high-pitched. She turned away at Luke's nar-

rowed gaze. 'It all needs a coat of paint, of course, and new carpet.'

'Or you could rip this carpet up and polish the existing floorboards.'

She shook her head. 'Lots of patients will have mobility problems. I'd want a non-slip surface. Water spilt on a carpet will be quickly absorbed, but wet floorboards could prove problematic for someone on crutches.'

He stared at her, admiration evident in those rich brown eyes of his. 'I'd never have thought about that.'

That admiration threatened to fluster her, so she added curtly, 'It's my job to think about it. Which brings me to another issue.' She led him back outside. 'I'll need wheelchair access—a ramp.'

He strode down the front steps and surveyed the veranda, hands on hips and legs planted wide. He paced the length of the front garden, bent down a couple of times to check... something. Keira tried not to notice how utterly masculine he looked, how completely assured and confident, but it tugged at her insides, softened her lower abdomen—and what had been cold warmed and filled with anticipation.

A burst of a child's laughter killed the warmth in a nanosecond. 'Mummy! Mummy! Watch this!'

Her head snapped back. Her shoulders drew in hard.

'You could have a ramp that extended from here—' Luke gestured to the front gate '—leading straight up to the veranda, or...'

From the corner of her eye she saw him move to the right. In the park opposite a group of children played tag—their high, thin voices and laughter made her chest cramp.

'Or you could have it running parallel from here, if you wanted an easier gradient.'

In the sun, the children's hair gleamed with good health. One of them started to sing 'Jingle Bells' and the others joined in. Her heart beat in time to the pain pounding behind her eyes. Her child should have had the chance to run like that, to sing like that. She should be the one sitting on this veranda watching her child and—

'Keira?'

She started when Luke touched her shoulder. The sympathy in his eyes burned acid in her chest. She jerked away, gestured to the imaginary ramp. 'I'm guessing John will be able to give me good advice about that?'

'Yep.'

Without another word, she turned on her heel and fled back inside, the children's laughter, their vitality, mocking her with a useless series of what-could-have-beens.

She hauled in a breath. It wasn't the children's fault. And it wasn't Luke's fault. He'd been everything that was generous and kind.

It's not your fault either.

She pushed the thought away. She couldn't go there.

She crossed into the front bedroom. 'I'm guessing you thought this would be the consulting room?'

He nodded. 'Is it big enough?'

'Plenty.' She kept her eyes averted from the front window. 'Desk here.' She pursed her lips and tried to concentrate. 'Examination table here, and a couple of chairs there...' And there would still be loads of room for exercises and whatnot.

It would be the perfect set up. For a clinic. Against her will, her eyes drifted towards the window.

'If you're as good as you've been saying, Keely...'

She could have hugged him for the teasing, the lightness, and the fact that it had her swinging away from the window. Only she couldn't hug him. Ever since their kiss down at the river last week, hugging Luke had become a decidedly bad idea. The thought of their bodies pressed up close against each other—his hardness, her softness, his strength seeping into her bones, the magic touch of his hands... She shook her head. Hugging Luke was off-limits. Unless she wanted it to lead to more kissing.

Of course she didn't want that!

She glanced at him. Or did she? Heat seared her skin when he turned and met her gaze.

She dragged hers away. Stop it! Her hormones had gone haywire. It was probably to be expected given…everything. Heaviness stole over her. That darkness threatened the edges of her vision.

She shrugged off the heaviness and lifted her chin. 'Oh, I'm as good as I say, Hillier.'

'Then you'll eventually have too much work for one person. You'll need to get in another physiotherapist or two to help cover the workload. That's why this house is so perfect.'

He led her back out to the corridor and along its length. 'Bedroom two and bedroom three—' he flung their doors open as they passed '—become consulting rooms two and three.'

She bit her lip. 'Where am I going to sleep? We are talking home business, aren't we?' He didn't mean for her to rent his room for ever?

The thought unnerved her, and she shot into the second bedroom. And ground to a halt, pressing a hand to her mouth. The first time she'd seen this house she'd thought this room would make the perfect nursery. A cot sitting in the middle of the room on an oriental rug, something soft and pastel on the walls, maybe a wallpaper border of nursery rhyme characters…

That life should have been hers!

'For the moment you'd sleep in one of these two rooms, but what I was thinking is down the track you'd put an extension on the back of the house. I'll show you what I mean.' He took her hand and led her across the corridor, through the dining room and into the kitchen.

The kitchen—the hub of the house. It should ring with

laughter and chatter. The same laughter and chatter that had filled the park. She'd imagined baking choc-chip cookies in this kitchen.

'You'd extend off the back like this.' He tugged her through the back door and out to the lawn. 'There'd be a big living/ family room here.'

Only she didn't have a family.

'And then a couple of bedrooms out this way.'

There should be a swing set there...and a sandpit.

'A big master bedroom here for you, and another smaller bedroom for your—'

He broke off when she flinched.

'And a spare bedroom there.' His voice sounded heavy as lead.

Perspiration broke out on her forehead, but her toes and fingers ached with cold. She couldn't help wondering if she'd gone as pale as he.

'I can't stand it,' she finally whispered. 'I know you're trying to help me see something good in the future, but...I can't stand it. Bedroom two was supposed to be a nursery.' She gestured to where she'd imagined the swing set and the sandpit. 'There were supposed to be birthday parties out here and...' Her throat closed over for a moment. 'I can't stand it, Luke.' The darkness loomed. 'I want to go back to Candlebark.'

She turned and strode around the side of the house. She couldn't bear to enter her great-aunt's home again, to walk through all its lovely rooms with all its lovely dreams.

That life should have been hers, but it had been snatched away. *Why?* That single word reverberated through her while she sat in the car and waited for Luke to lock up.

Why?

When he slid behind the driver's seat, he didn't start the car up immediately. She gripped her hands together and met his gaze.

His eyes were dark. Those grooves bit deep either side of his mouth. 'Keira, I'm sorry. I should've thought—'

'No! No, Luke—you were trying to help. I know that. You've been a good friend. I'm the one who's sorry.'

'You have nothing to be sorry for.'

Pain stretched behind her eyes. For most of the last year she'd eaten good wholesome food, taken all the vitamins her doctor had recommended, avoided caffeine and alcohol. She'd made sure that she'd exercised and that she got a little sun most days—not a lot, just a bit. She'd done all the things that would help her fall pregnant, and all the things that, once pregnant, would nourish her baby. *It wasn't fair that the miscarriage had happened to her!*

Anger ripped through her. She tried to cram it down deep inside her. Luke didn't deserve her anger. 'Please, Luke, can we just go back to the farm?'

Without another word he started the car and turned it in the direction of Candlebark. She was grateful he didn't try to make small talk on the journey home. It gave her a chance to concentrate on stifling the anger roaring through her, threatening to flare out of control and scorch all within its path.

She'd endured almost a year of IVF treatment before she'd finally fallen pregnant—endless drugs, endless procedures, nail-biting waits—all for what?

A low growl crouched in her throat. When Luke brought the ute to a halt in its usual spot by the barn, she shoved her door open and tried to leap out. But she'd forgotten to undo her seatbelt. She tugged at it furiously, that growl emerging low and guttural. Luke leaned across and released the catch.

She fell out, stumbled to her knees before lurching to her feet again. Spinning around, she slammed the car door shut and set off towards the house.

'Keira?'

She stopped to shake an unsteady forefinger at him. 'I am so angry, Luke, but *you* don't deserve to bear the brunt of it.'

She had to get out of his presence before she did something unforgivable. 'You have been lovely—utterly lovely! I'm not angry with you!'

She kicked at a tuft of grass, and then she moved up to the paling fence and slapped it—hard. Pain shot through her hand and up her arm in a satisfying wave, making it possible to ignore the ache in her chest for a tenth of a second. She clenched her hand to a fist, drew it back...

'Whoa!' Before she could punch the fence, Luke's large, warm hand closed over hers, his other arm going about her waist and lifting her bodily off the ground.

She tried to struggle free. 'Put me down, Luke. I want to smash something!'

'I know.'

'Don't try and stop me. I—'

'I'm not.'

She stopped struggling. He was taking her towards the barn. 'You're not?'

'No, but I'm not going to let you break your hand either.' His voice was grim. 'I think we've both had enough of hospitals for the moment, don't you?'

Anger hot and untempered rushed through her. 'I'll be happy if I never see another hospital as long as I live,' she bit out.

'Good.'

He didn't set her down until they were deep inside the barn. That was when she saw it, hanging from a low beam—a punching bag. She laughed, but her laugh didn't contain an ounce of mirth.

Intent, she moved towards it, but Luke grabbed her wrist and pulled her to a halt. 'Put these on first.' He handed her a set of thin leather gloves. They weren't boxing gloves, but she didn't care. She reefed them on and started towards the bag again.

A growl of rage—a sound she hadn't known she was

capable of making—emerged from her throat when Luke
pulled her to another halt. 'What *now*?' she all but yelled at
him.

'That bag—it's heavy. It won't move much when you punch
it. That can be...unsatisfying.' He held a wooden baseball bat
out to her. 'Try hitting it with this.'

She gritted her teeth and took the bat. 'Excellent.'

She moved in close to the punching bag, drew the bat back,
and then let fly with all her might. It hit with a dull thud, and
the force of it vibrated through her arms and into her shoulders, making the bag shudder.

That's for my stupid body, with its ovary on the blink!

She drew the bat back and took another swing. *Thud!* It
set the bag swaying.

*That's for making me wait almost a year before falling
pregnant!*

Wind up, swing...thud.

And that's for making me lose my baby!

She stared at the swaying, juddering punching bag and her
legs started to tremble. The anger slid out of her and the bat
slipped from her fingers. She backed up to a hay bale and sat,
breathing hard.

'Did you hurt yourself?'

Luke was there, drawing off her gloves. She shook her
head.

'Keira?'

'The miscarriage.' She swallowed. 'It wasn't my fault.'

'No.'

'It's...it's not fair that I lost my baby.'

'I know.'

Her face crumpled. She'd lost her baby—her beautiful
baby—and all the plans she'd made for it.

She hauled in a breath and did her best to smooth out her
face, to push the pain, the darkness, away. But her face refused
to co-operate, and the pain beat at her, breaking over her in

wave after wave, making her head bow and her shoulders shake.

The constriction around her chest tightened. She couldn't draw breath. She knew the moment she did her defences would fall. She tried to hold it, but the burning in her lungs built and stretched and scalded her until she couldn't fight it any longer.

A sob burst from her. She dropped her face to her hands, her entire body shaking. Arms went about her, holding her and rocking her. Luke. His breath warm at her temple and his arms strong, supporting her as the sobs engulfed her. Being held in his arms didn't make up for losing her baby—not one little bit—but it did help, which made her cry harder for a bit. Being here with him like this helped a lot.

When her tears had finally spent themselves she lay in his arms, tired beyond belief. 'You want to know what one of the hardest things is?' she finally whispered.

'Tell me.'

'In the eyes of the world, my baby was nothing.' She dragged in a shuddering breath, incapable of any other movement at the moment. 'I feel as bereaved as if my baby had been stillborn, and yet I can't even have a service for it. I can't honour it in that way and—'

She didn't know the words to express how bad that made her feel. When she glanced up into his eyes, though, she knew she didn't have to. He understood.

And that helped too. A little.

When they returned to the house, Luke opened the back door to discover Christmas carols belting out from the sound system in the living room.

He closed his eyes with a grimace. He knew what he and Jason had decided, and in principle he'd agreed with it. At the moment, though, it seemed the worse timing possible.

He strode through to the living room and made silent

motions, drawing his hand across his neck and shaking his head. Jason immediately leapt to his feet and all but dived across the room to hit the stop button.

'No—don't. Not on my account.'

Luke swallowed. He hadn't realised Keira had followed so close behind him. Jason hovered by the sound system and glanced from Luke to Keira, and then back at his dad. Luke didn't know what to tell him, so he simply settled for a shrug. Keira sat. Jason contented himself with turning the volume down a couple of notches, and joined Keira on the sofa.

She glanced up at Luke. 'I told you—I *like* Christmas carols.'

He found he didn't quite know what to do with his hands and his feet. That hadn't been a problem when Keira had been crying. He'd just held her, and ached right alongside her. 'I know, but I wasn't sure you'd find them appropriate today.'

'Why not? It *is* Christmas.'

He shuffled his feet, shoved his hands into his pockets. Keira and Jason looked comfortable, sitting on the sofa like that. Jason sprawled at one end in his typical lounging, slouching fashion. Keira rested her head back against the sofa's softness at the other end.

She turned to glance at Jason. 'You like Christmas carols?'

He grinned. 'Only when my mates aren't around.'

It hit Luke then that they looked like a family.

He tried to kill the thought before it could fully form. No peace—not for anyone—could be found in it.

Another thought followed swiftly on its heels—he wanted to be sitting there on the sofa with them. There was room. It was a large sofa. He forced himself towards an armchair instead. He tried to push all thoughts of warmth and softness and the scent of vanilla from his mind. What he wanted was neither here nor there. What he should be focusing on was Keira and her wellbeing.

He tried to study her as surreptitiously as he could. She was pale, and her eyes were red-rimmed, but she seemed calmer, steadier than she had been in the last three days. Letting out all that anger, followed by the crying jag—her acknowledgement of her grief—he knew was only the beginning of her grieving process. But if he and Jason could give her a nice Christmas—nothing fancy, just a bit of company and some fun—then maybe that would help her heal just a little bit more.

It was the least he could do after hauling her off to her great-aunt's house like he'd done. That had been a serious error of judgement. He'd thought it might provide her with something else to focus on—a new project. He bit back an oath when he recalled the stark whiteness of her face, the misery haunting her eyes. He should be shot for putting her through that.

His mouth dried. He should be shot because he'd pushed her so hard to set up her clinic in Gunnedah, because he wanted her to stay. It was as simple as that.

All the strength left his body, his back slumping in the armchair, his head suddenly too heavy for his neck. Keira smiled at him as if she understood exactly how he felt.

Tension shot through him. He couldn't let her misinterpret his actions. He couldn't let her rely on him for more than friendship. He'd told her it was okay to rely on other people and he'd meant it. As long as she didn't count *him* as other people.

He would let her down.

To be free to love a woman like Keira, to build a family with her—whatever shape that family took—was what he wanted more than life itself.

But he couldn't have it. A man like him couldn't be trusted with a woman's heart. Especially not a woman as loving and giving as Keira. If he ever saw the hurt and disappointment that he'd caused in Tammy spring into Keira's eyes... It would tear him to pieces inside.

She deserved better. Much better. So had Tammy. He would not risk Keira's happiness for his own selfish needs.

'So, I guess you'll be putting your great-aunt's house on the market like you always meant to?' He made his voice brusque and businesslike.

The light in her eyes faded. He told himself this was the wise thing to do, sensible—to erect a wall that would protect her from his faithless heart. 'You'll have Christmas with us at Candlebark, sell the house, and then return to the city, where Gunnedah will become a faint memory.'

She suddenly smiled, as if she'd worked out the subtext to his words. 'Are you trying to tell me that you'll miss me?'

Hell, no! Even if the answer to that question was a resounding *yes*!

'If you invite me to visit, I'll come,' she said.

'Sweet,' said Jason.

'You'll be welcome any time.' Luke made his voice deliberately neutral—polite. It made the frown spring back into her eyes.

When she left, he'd allow himself the comfort of a couple of phone calls—just to make sure she was okay—but he wouldn't invite her to visit and she wouldn't suggest it. The time between phone calls would lengthen until they eventually dwindled to nothing. He'd make sure of it. In the long run it was what would be easier for everyone.

'To be honest, Luke, I have to admit I'm not focusing on anything much beyond Christmas.'

He was pushing her again! His hands clenched. Just because he couldn't get the thought of holding her, touching her, kissing her, out of his head, it didn't mean she felt the same way.

Selfish—that was what he was, he suddenly realised. Because the boundaries were for *him*—for his benefit, his

protection. He ground his teeth together. He shouldn't be concerned with anything other than providing her with whatever
she needed while she remained at Candlebark. Not with what
would be best and easiest for him.

In his heart he knew she'd return to the city. She knew that
she didn't belong with him.

He would give her Christmas…and there was one more
thing he could do for her too.

In the eyes of the world, my baby was nothing.

His jaw locked for a moment. He unlocked it to ask, 'Keira,
do you have a favourite poem?'

She cocked her head to one side. 'My favourite poet is
Robert Frost. *The Road Not Taken* was my mother's favourite
poem. What about you?'

'Banjo Patterson's *Clancy of the Overflow.*'

She turned to Jason. 'Anything by Spike Milligan,' he said
promptly.

He reeled off a nonsense verse that had sudden laughter
rising through Luke. 'You used to recite that when you were
five or six.'

Keira smiled. It was slow, but it had the same impact as
the sun coming out from behind a bank of stormclouds. Luke
couldn't look away as she recited a nonsense verse back at
Jason. Then she and Jason shot nonsense verse back and forth
until they both started to laugh.

Luke rested his head back and feasted his eyes on the
sight. It was beyond anything to see some of her vivacity and
colour returning. It eased something inside him to hear his
son laughing.

'Oh, that was fun!' Keira turned back to Luke. 'But what
on earth made you ask such a question?'

'Oh…uh…a poetry programme I caught on the radio,' he
improvised, recalled to his original purpose. 'What's your
favourite plant?'

'Let me guess—you caught a gardening programme on the radio too?'

'Every Saturday morning from eight till nine.'

'No prizes for guessing yours, I suppose?'

'Wheat,' he and Jason said in unison.

'There's lots and lots that I love. Flowers are wonderful, but scents are the best. And my favourite smelling plant is…'

She flipped out several fingers. Luke found himself leaning towards her, elbows resting on knees. 'What are you deciding between?'

'Freesias and frangipani…'

Heck, where would he get a frangipani tree out here?

'Gardenias… Oh, and roses, of course.'

'Of course,' he echoed. He could do a rosebush.

'Wattle,' she finally decided. 'Wattle is my favourite plant. It smells divine, and it looks wonderful.'

He filed that information away.

She stared at him for several moments, as if awaiting another out of the blue question. 'What? Not going to ask me my favourite song?' she teased.

He straightened. He hadn't thought of that. 'Yeah.'

But with a laugh and a shake of her head she turned to Jason. 'What's your favourite Christmas memory?'

'That's easy.'

Luke's head shot up. It was?

'The year I was seven I woke up really, really early to find Santa had left me a bike.'

The breath whooshed out of Luke as the memory swept over him. 'Man, you should've heard him. He made enough noise to wake the neighbours.'

'Dad took me down to the local park, probably so Mum could sleep in, and he taught me how to ride it. It was brilliant! I fell over a lot, but it didn't matter, 'cos the grass was soft. And Dad would always pick me up, dust me off, and away we'd go again.'

Luke remembered that morning and grinned. At seven, Jason had had boundless energy.

'And when we got home Mum was cooking blueberry pancakes, and I remember this huge glazed ham sitting on the table. One of my other presents was this compendium of board games, and I think we ate and played board games and watched Christmas stuff on the telly all day. And then on Boxing Day we got up really early and drove here. Candlebark was my favourite place in the world.' Jason paused. 'So that Christmas I got the best presents and we had the best fun...and I knew that the next day I'd be going to my favourite place.'

'That's a great memory,' Keira said.

'It was a beaut Christmas,' Luke agreed.

And it had been. But a few short years later Luke had destroyed all that. He'd made promises he couldn't keep. Tammy hadn't deserved that, and neither had Jason.

He glanced at Keira and resolution gelled in his stomach. He would do all he could to make this Christmas special for her, but he wouldn't make her any promises. He wasn't the kind of man who could be trusted to keep his word.

CHAPTER TEN

ON WEDNESDAY morning, four days after her miscarriage, Luke set a beautifully carved oak box on the table beside her cereal bowl. Keira stared at it, and wondered how long before she stopped counting off the days.

'What's this?'

She glanced up at Luke. Just for a moment he looked touchingly uncertain. She didn't know what it was about his rich brown eyes that could have her melting into a puddle in no more than the blink of an eye.

He crouched down beside her. 'Keira, I don't think your baby was nothing. Neither does Jason. What you said about not being able to have any kind of memorial service—that struck me as pretty important. If Jason and I hadn't been able to have a service for Tammy I don't know how we could've moved on.'

She abandoned her cereal to lean back and press both hands to her chest.

'Jason and I thought that if it's okay with you, if it's something you'd like to do, we could hold a service in the garden for your baby. I know it's not the same as one in a church or a cemetery, but...we'd like to honour your baby, to remember it. But only if that's okay with you.'

Her eyes filled, and hot tears spilled onto her cheeks. For a moment she couldn't say anything. Finally, she nodded. 'I'd like that very much...thank you.'

'Both of us wanted to give your baby something…a token.' He leant out to stroke the box with one tanned finger. 'This held all my boyhood treasures.' He set a carved ebony figurine of a horse beside it. 'And this was Jason's most treasured possession when he was younger.' He added a spray of rosemary to the pile without another word.

Rosemary for remembrance…

Her face crumpled. She buried her face in the hanky he handed her. When she was sure of herself again, she lifted her face, blew her nose, and stared at those simple treasures. 'That's very kind of you and Jason.'

'I figured you might like to add one or two things of your own.' He rose when she nodded. 'We'll be out in the garden when you're ready.'

Keira placed the three sets of knitted booties she'd bought from the women's auxiliary stall, a Christmas bib she hadn't been able to resist buying when she'd been waiting for the estate agent one day, and the most colourful of the pictures books, into the oak box. She added the horse and the rosemary. With a kiss, she sealed it. Then she put on her prettiest summer dress and joined Luke and Jason in the garden.

The service was simple but it poured balm on the wound stretching across her heart. Luke said a few words about how much her baby had been wanted and loved…and how much it would be missed. Then he read out a Robert Frost poem, and it was perfect. So perfect that for a moment she couldn't see because tears made the garden blur. Jason read a psalm from the bible, and then Luke pressed a button on the portable CD player he had sitting nearby and the sweet strains of 'Amazing Grace' filled the garden.

They all sang—not always in key—but Keira didn't care. A fierce love for her baby and for the two males standing either side of her filled her. When the hymn came to an end Luke gestured, and she placed the oak box with all their treasures into the fresh earth Luke and Jason had turned over. And then they covered it in and planted a wattle tree to mark the spot.

'Thank you,' she whispered, glancing up at Luke. 'You don't know how much this means to me.'

Luke's brown-eyed gaze told her he knew exactly what it meant.

They returned to the house and drank coffee, and ate a tea bun that Keira realised Luke must have bought fresh from town that morning.

'Right,' he said when they were finished, 'now we're going to make a boiled fruitcake.'

Both Keira's and Jason's jaws dropped. 'But,' she started, 'don't you have work to do?'

'Yep, I have a fruitcake to make.' When she opened her mouth he shook his head. 'There's a few chores I'll have to take care of later this afternoon, but that's hours away yet. Besides, Jason will help me with them—won't you?'

'Sure I will.'

He didn't want to leave her alone to mope herself into a depression after that memorial service, she realised. His ongoing thoughtfulness touched her more deeply than she suspected it should. She shrugged that thought off. 'But...a boiled fruitcake?'

'I know we've left it a bit late, but Christmas isn't complete without fruitcake.'

She started to laugh. 'I won't argue with that.'

'And when you were talking about Christmas memories the other day I suddenly remembered that every year I'd help my mother make a boiled fruitcake. It was always a bit of an event.'

She was glad he had at least one good Christmas memory. She watched him dig out mixing bowls from a cupboard. He handed her a sheet of paper. 'That's her recipe.' He handed Jason a measuring cup before planting himself in front of the pantry. 'You better start by reading out the list of ingredients.'

She read the items out one by one, and Luke retrieved them. Jason, reading over her shoulder, started measuring ingredients into bowls. She grabbed a wooden spoon and helped to mix. At some stage Luke put on the CD of Christmas carols and Keira lost herself in the simple pleasure of easy conversation, humming along to old favourites and making a cake.

At some point it filtered into her that she would always mourn the loss of her baby, that she would never stop missing her Munchkin and all that could have been. Motherhood might be closed to her, but it didn't mean life still couldn't be good. At least…bits of it. Like Christmas.

Luke nudged her with a friendly shoulder. 'You okay?'

'Sure.' She pasted on a smile and pushed her sombre reflections aside. To help this man and his son have their first good Christmas in three years—that would give her more satisfaction than anything else at the moment. 'I…' She gestured. 'This is fun.'

'Yeah, it is,' he said, as if it had taken him by surprise too.

That was when it hit her that she needed a Christmas miracle, because she'd gone and done the unthinkable—she'd fallen in love with Luke Hillier.

She swallowed. That was crazy nonsense! It was her haywire hormones and nothing more.

Still, it was Christmas. And if she needed a miracle Christmas was the time to ask for one.

Keira knew the exact moment Luke stopped in the living room doorway, but she didn't turn around. Her growing awareness for the man continued to disconcert her—especially as she received such conflicting signals from Luke himself.

At times he was utterly concerned and solicitous about her welfare, making sure she wanted for nothing, quietly watching to make sure she ate enough and that she didn't physically push herself too hard. It made her feel like a princess, a queen. It made her feel not alone. It made her feel…loved.

At other times, though, he was distant, gruff, almost abrupt, as if he were out of patience with her.

And then there were those times when his gaze fastened on her mouth and his eyes would darken, his hands would clench, and something inside Keira would stir to languorous life and hold its breath, waiting for him to kiss her.

He never did.

And she couldn't get the memory of their one kiss out of her mind. The feel of all that firm flesh beneath her fingertips, the rightness of his lips on hers. That kiss had transported her to a place she hadn't known existed—beyond desire to a one-on-one harmony that had made her spirit soar. Her soul hungered to experience it again.

Her lips twisted. Who was she trying to kid? She wanted to seize hold of it and never let go. Luke had experienced the desire, but that soul-to-soul togetherness hadn't reached out and stroked him with its enchanted fingertips. If it had he wouldn't be able to resist kissing her again and trying to recreate it.

So…all in all, it was just as well he didn't kiss her. And the sooner she forgot about kissing the better!

If only she could get her stupid body to believe that. And her traitor of a heart.

Maybe he's giving you time to heal after your miscarriage?

She crushed an almost hysterical desire to laugh. She was leaving for the city next week. Time was the one thing they didn't have.

She bit back a sigh and refused to turn around, even though Luke's presence beat at her and made her skin itch and prickle.

Jason, though, showed no such reticence as he brushed past

Luke to get more staples from Luke's office. 'Hey, Dad, what do you think?'

This morning she and Jason had gone shopping. They'd bought all the ingredients for Christmas dinner, and some odds and ends to make Christmas decorations. She'd wanted to prove to Luke that Christmas didn't have to cost a lot of money. So this afternoon she and Jason were making angel chains and Christmas lanterns from shiny foil paper and hanging them as they went. Their handiwork draped the mantelpiece, hung from each of the windows, and festooned the French doors that lead out to the veranda.

'It…uh…looks very festive.'

She finished cutting out her row of angels. Only then did she allow herself to turn and survey Luke's face. He stared around a bit dazed, but not in a bad way, she decided. He just needed to lighten up and let his hair down for a bit.

A ripple of mischief squirmed through her. She grabbed a wad of tack and rose, moving to where Luke slouched in the doorway. 'Here—you can help me.' She handed him one end of her angel chain and pointed to the top of the doorframe. He obediently reached up and pressed it into place, giving Keira a pleasing eyeful of broad shoulder and rippling muscle as he did so.

'My turn.' She stood on tiptoe, one hand on Luke's shoulder for balance as she reached above her head. One of Luke's hands automatically went to the small of her back to steady her, and it felt so good there she took her time fixing her foil angels into place.

'Are you almost finished?' he eventually ground out.

It made her grin. 'Not quite.'

With a flourish she pulled a spray of mistletoe from her pocket and dangled it above their heads. 'Know what this is?'

He scowled. 'Mistletoe.'

His utter lack of enthusiasm made her laugh. She tacked it

into place. When she was done, his hand immediately dropped from her waist, but she left her hand resting on his shoulder. 'Oh, no, you don't, Luke Hillier. Not so fast. You've been caught under the mistletoe.'

His jaw dropped. 'But...but that's cheating!'

'Face it, Luke.' She drew her hand down from his shoulder to his chest in a slow, lingering curve, relishing every contour and the way his muscles tightened at her touch. Beneath her palm his heart thudded, and the hot male feel of him branded itself on her skin. 'You're going to have to kiss the lodger.'

He really did need to lighten up. She shimmied in closer, lifted her face. 'C'mon, you can do it.' She sent him her cheek-iest grin and pointed to her cheek. 'Right there, Hillier.'

Her grin faded, however, as Luke lifted one large hand and curved it around the back of her head, his thumb running lightly back and forth over the pulse at the side of her throat. 'You like playing with fire, Keely?'

His eyes darkened. His lips—those sure, firm lips—parted as if to allow him to draw more breath into his lungs. Oh, dear Lord! Her pulse went mad and the strength drained from her limbs. Her hand fisted into the cotton of his shirt as his mouth descended.

He pressed the lightest of kisses to the side of her neck, just below her ear, his breath teasing her overheated flesh as his mouth moved to her cheek. 'Here? Is this where you meant, Keely?'

She tried to nod, but she couldn't move. She could barely swallow as that thumb moved back and forth. Back and forth over that pulse point in a barely there skin-on-skin touch until need screamed through her. Just by the touch of his thumb!

And the warm pressure of his hand curling around her scalp.

And the dark promise in his eyes.

And those wicked lips.

'I consider myself more of a traditionalist, however.'

Those sinful lips curved upwards and her breath hitched. 'I prefer lip-on-lip contact.'

Oh, he couldn't mean—

He touched his lips to the corner of her mouth. Her knees shook. He touched his lips to the other corner, lingering until white-hot tendrils whipped through her. He drew back, gazed at her long and hard, as if he meant to savour every single moment of the lip-on-lip contact he'd promised, and it drew her as taut as a newly strung bow. With agonising slowness he eased forward again. His lips brushed hers, feather-light, magical, and then he eased back, just as her lips opened in an attempt to deepen the fleeting caress. He grinned down at her, as if he knew exactly what havoc he'd played on her senses.

'How was that, Keely? Pass muster?'

She straightened, swallowed, and unclenched her hand from the cotton of his shirt. 'You better watch yourself, Hillier.' She smoothed the cotton out. 'I'll be spending the rest of Christmas trying to catch you beneath the mistletoe.'

He threw his head back and laughed. 'I consider myself duly warned. Now, enough of this seasonal silliness.' He smiled as Jason came back in with a box of staples. 'I need the pair of you to help me unload the car.'

Keira and Jason stared at each other, and then at him.

'I...uh...' He shuffled his feet and looked deliciously out of his depth. He waved a hand at the decorations she and Jason had made. 'It appears that great minds think alike,' he muttered.

With that, he strode from the room. Keira hesitated for half a second before following him out through the back door and down the steps towards the barn, doing what she could to get her hormones back under some semblance of control. All around her the wheat waved golden in the fields. High in the sky cirrus clouds traced tracks of foam. In two days it would be Christmas...and Luke had just kissed her! She jumped up and high-fived a branch in a nearby bottlebrush tree.

Luke halted by the tray of the ute. She stopped beside him—not too close—and peered inside. 'A Christmas tree?' And by the look of its box it must have been the biggest one he could find.

Jason peered over her shoulder. 'Sweet!'

She'd wanted to buy one when she and Jason had been shopping earlier, but had been afraid of overstepping some unspoken boundary.

Luke glanced at her from beneath a lock of hair that had fallen forward onto his forehead. 'Is it...um...okay?'

'It's better than okay!' She couldn't help it. She turned and hugged him. Hard. Then she let him go, because neither she nor her body had forgotten that episode beneath the mistletoe yet. 'It's perfect!'

She stared down at the Christmas tree, and all the associated bags and boxes of tinsel and decorations. 'My favourite Christmas memory is decorating the tree with my mother every year.'

Luke planted his hands on his hips. 'Why didn't you say something sooner?'

She shrugged and risked glancing up at him. 'It didn't seem right, somehow.' But now... 'Ooh, c'mon—let's unload it.' She clapped her hands. 'Time's a-wasting.'

The genuine delight on Keira's face as they set up the Christmas tree lightened Luke's heart. A Christmas tree—such a small thing—but it gave her so much joy.

Mistletoe was an even smaller thing, he reminded himself with a wry twist of his lips, but it had nearly undone him. For a brief crazy moment her teasing had made him feel young again. He had to take serious care he didn't get stuck under that mistletoe with her again.

'Have some shortbread.' Keira held a plate out towards him, humming along to 'Deck the Halls' as it blasted out from the CD-player.

He took a break from unknotting tinsel to select a piece. He bit into the crumbly sweetness and then had to close his eyes against the vivid need that shook through him. He couldn't let all this go to his head—Keira handing out traditional Christmas treats and singing along to carols while she helped his son decorate the tree, and both of them turning to him every now and again to tell him what a stroke of genius the tree was—none of it was real.

Well, it *was* real, he amended, but it fed too closely into the fantasy. A fantasy that could never come true. This was a mirage—a temporary illusion. In a few days Keira would be gone, and she'd leave a gap in his life. He had no illusions about that. All the same, he would do nothing to stop her from leaving. He'd promote it if he had to.

If she stayed he would break her heart—just as he'd broken Tammy's. He'd make her promises he couldn't keep—just as he had with Tammy. Keira's eyes might go all soft now, when they rested on him, but if she stayed eventually they'd harden with disappointment and heartbreak. He'd put lines of care on her face.

He couldn't stand the thought of doing that. Better she left in a few days than they risk exploring the heights he instinctively knew they could scale together. Her eventual pain would not be worth it. It would be a thousand times better that he suffer the torment now than for her to suffer it later.

In the meantime, he had to work at keeping things light.

And no more kissing under the mistletoe!

'Earth to Luke?'

He crashed back to find Keira holding out a large golden star.

'You can do the honours.' And she pointed to the top of the tree.

'Me?'

'Yes, you. You were the one to surprise us so wonderfully in the first place, and…'

'And?' he asked, intrigued in spite of himself.

'And you're the only one tall enough to reach the top.'

He grinned and popped the rest of his shortbread into his mouth, wiped his fingers on his jeans and carefully took the star. He settled it into place, securing it there as gently as he could and doing his best not to dislodge any of the other decorations.

He stepped back to survey their handiwork.

'Sweet,' Jason said, moving in beside him.

'Perfect,' Keira breathed from his other side.

And just for a moment while he stared at the tree he had a glimpse of the true spirit of the season, and it eased the ache out of his chest.

'It really does feel like Christmas now,' Keira added with a satisfied sigh, and his chest expanded. His plan had worked, but it hadn't just lifted *her* spirits. It had lifted Jason's too. *Even teenagers need Christmas.* He vowed that in the future he wouldn't forget.

He stepped back before the fantasy could swallow the last shred of his sanity. 'Is there anything else we need to make Christmas perfect?' Tomorrow was Christmas Eve. That meant there was only one more shopping day left.

'I don't think so.' Keira sucked her bottom lip into her mouth before letting it go again. It glistened as bright as the tinsel and the foil angels that swayed in the breeze from the French doors. For the life of him, Luke couldn't look away. 'We've bought enough food to feed an army!'

'We're roasting a turkey and vegetables,' Jason said, practically drooling as he threw himself down on the sofa. 'Keira promised to show me how to cook it so we can make it next year.'

When Keira wouldn't be here.

Luke retreated to his armchair and pretended to admire the Christmas tree.

'And we have all the ingredients for a pavlova.'

From her tone, pavlova must be one of her all-time favourite things.

'Not to mention enough chocolate-coated sultanas, short-bread, sweets and nuts to sink a ship.'

'And fruitcake,' he added, remembering how they'd made that cake—the easy laughter and camaraderie.

'And fruitcake,' she agreed.

She settled herself in the other armchair, the one furthest from him and nearest the Christmas tree. Her hair curved around her face. He curled his hands into fists, but that didn't stop him remembering its softness. She wore the same shorts she had the day she'd paddled in the river—the day of their picnic. The day they'd—

She crossed her legs, her shorts rode up, and he forced himself to glance away.

He saw Jason surveying the tree with eyes that glowed and his heart clenched. He would never be able to thank Keira for bringing Christmas back into his son's life. He had to clear his throat before trusting himself to speak. 'Are you spending Christmas night with your grandparents?'

'Dunno.'

Something about his tone had Luke straightening. Now that he came to think about it, Jason hadn't spent any time at all with Brenda and Alf this last week. 'You want to tell me about it?'

Jason shrugged. 'We had words,' he mumbled. 'I told them they had to stop saying bad things about you in front of me—that I didn't want to hear it. I told them they were wrong about you, and that you did love Mum even if it wasn't the way they wanted you to.'

Luke stilled.

'I told them to get back to me when they'd worked out if they could do that or not.'

'Aw, hell, son, I…' He swallowed, and tried to tell Jason how much Brenda and Alf needed him, but he choked up.

Keira spoke over the top of him anyway. 'Good for you. They'll come around—you'll see.'

Did she really think so?

'Yeah, I reckon they will too.'

Luke gazed at them both in astonishment.

'Don't sweat it, Dad.'

Jason clambered to his feet, and it hit Luke just how much his son had grown up in the last couple of years. 'Do you have any idea how much you sounded like your mother just then?'

A grin spread across Jason's face. 'Yeah? Sweet! I'm going to exercise Dusty.' With that, he pushed out through the French doors, whistling.

Luke swung back to Keira. 'But Brenda and Alf...' His heart went out to them. They'd lost their only child. Their grief and anger—he understood it only too well.

'Jason has a right to ask the adults in his life to act in a reasonable manner.'

He closed his mouth. She was right.

'And maybe this is the shake-up Brenda and Alf need. They won't find any peace in the bitterness they keep perpetuating. They need to concern themselves with the living, not with the dead. It's time they started remembering all the good things about Tammy, instead of focussing on her death and the gap she's left behind.'

He couldn't help but stare at her. She brushed a strand of hair back behind her ear and shrugged, not quite meeting his eye. 'My gran told me all that when my mother died.'

His heart ached at how much she'd lost and how alone in the world she was. 'Keira, your coming to Candlebark was a stroke of good fortune for Jason and I.' He paused. 'I just wish it could've been as good and as trouble-free for you.'

She glanced away. 'My miscarriage had nothing to do with your farm, Luke, or the town of Gunnedah.'

There was something in the way she said it that suddenly

froze his blood. Something hard and unrelenting in her voice that he hadn't heard there before. He shot forward to the edge of his seat. 'When you return to the city, Keira, you will be pursuing your IVF treatment, won't you?'

She shrugged, but still didn't look at him. 'I kind of think the universe has spoken up on that subject, Luke, don't you?'

His gut clenched. So did his hands. 'You can't give up on your dream of becoming a mother!' The words burst from him.

She turned then, and met his gaze. 'It's too soon to think about it.' Her eyes were dark and shadowed. 'I don't want to talk about it, Luke. Please—it's Christmas.'

And he had promised her Christmas. He nodded, but his heart burned in protest.

She sagged. 'Thank you. Now...' She straightened again. 'What gifts have you bought for Jason?'

'I...uh...' He shifted on his chair. 'None.'

'None!' She stared at him, evidently scandalised. Then her face softened. 'Let me guess, Tammy used to take care of that side of things?'

He nodded.

She sucked her bottom lip into her mouth. 'Didn't you and your family exchange gifts when you were growing up?'

When he was very little he seemed to recall there'd been some gifts. After that... 'We had dreadful droughts out here during the eighties. There wasn't much spare cash. Everything we had went back into the farm or to the bank.'

She sucked that bottom lip into her mouth again. He wished she'd stop doing that. As if she'd heard that thought rattling around in his head, she suddenly pursed them instead, and he could have groaned out loud—that wasn't any better!

'What about now?'

Was she asking him if he had enough money to buy Jason a Christmas present?

'We're a bit cash-poor until the harvest comes in. Once it does, though…' They were on track to make a tidy profit this year. 'I can afford a gift or two, if that's what you're asking.' This should have occurred to him sooner. He scratched his head. What did one get a fourteen—nearly fifteen—year-old boy for Christmas these days? What had he wanted when he was fourteen?

Again, as if she could read his mind, she gestured towards the television unit. 'I see that Jason has one of those game consoles.' She paused and her eyes suddenly twinkled. 'Unless that's yours, of course?'

Two weeks ago he'd barely been able to crack a smile. Now she could have him grinning as easy as not.

Two weeks ago he'd have dreaded going into town. Today he hadn't given it a second thought. He'd just wanted to buy Keira and Jason a Christmas tree.

Presents, though, had completely slipped his mind.

'Well,' she started, 'I have it on very good authority that the hottest game this year has something to do with dragons… and the Gunnedah Games Shop has it in stock.'

He gazed at her in admiration. 'You're good.'

'I am.'

She said it with such deadpan seriousness he burst out laughing. 'Jason told you, huh?'

'I believe you're accusing me of cheating, Hillier. Indeed he did—but not quite in the way you think. When we walked past the Games Shop earlier today he hollered, "Sweet!" and pressed his face up against the window like a little boy.'

Her description somehow had Luke's gut tightening and melting both at the same time.

'And then there are the staple presents to fall back on, of course.'

'Staple presents?'

She nodded. 'There are the unisex chocolates and sweets. Then for men it's socks and undies. Every male should get those on Christmas and birthdays. Women are convinced that men are incapable of buying them on their own, you see.'

He knew she was teasing him. 'And what are the female equivalents?'

'Body lotions and bath bombs. Men know that women like to smell good.'

She didn't have any problem in that department—she smelt great! Still, he vowed then and there to get her some kind of body pamper-pack—vanilla-scented, of course.

The phone suddenly rang. Luke blinked. It took him a moment to realise what the sound was as it was such a rare event. And not a welcome one, he acknowledged as he hauled himself out of his chair. He'd have gladly idled away the rest of the afternoon chatting with Keira.

He ground his teeth together. All in all it was probably just as well they'd been interrupted.

'Hello?'

A cool, professional female voice asked to speak to Keira. Wordlessly, he held the phone out towards his house guest.

Keira immediately leapt to her feet, and sent him a puzzled glance before taking the receiver. 'Hello?'

Her frown cleared immediately when she realised who was on the other end, so Luke moved back to his chair and tried not to study her too closely, tried not to pay attention to her conversation.

'Oh, so soon?'

He had about as much chance of that as he did of getting the entire harvest in this afternoon. His gaze narrowed in on the way she worried at her bottom lip.

'No—no, of course not. If that's your professional opinion then I'll take your advice. You're the expert.' She swallowed. 'I'm glad there's so much interest.'

She didn't look glad.

'I just thought it would take a whole lot longer. This is… good news.'

Then why was she frowning?

'I'll pop in tomorrow. Yes—thanks, Julia.'

She replaced the receiver. She stood by the phone for a long moment, and then pasted on a smile that didn't quite reach her eyes. All his muscles tensed. 'Is everything okay?'

'That was my new estate agent. She said there's been a lot of interest in my great-aunt's house.'

Of course there had. It was a great house.

'She wants to take it to auction on the twenty-ninth of this month, while interest is running hot.'

He let out a low whistle.

'Is it okay if I stay here till then?'

'Not a problem at all. Stay until everything is settled.' He paused. 'It's moving very fast.'

She nodded.

'Are you sure you're ready for this?'

She lifted her chin. 'It's what I came here to do.'

And when it was done she would leave, and there would be no reason for her to ever return. He pressed his lips together and rose. 'I better get onto the chores.'

'Yes, of course.'

The scent of vanilla followed him all the way out to the barn.

CHAPTER ELEVEN

KEIRA woke early on Christmas morning. She tried to push her wakefulness away, and drag the mantle of sleep back over her, but as happened every Christmas morning the thrill of excitement threading through her made that impossible. As it had every Christmas morning for as long as she could remember.

Even those Christmases when she'd ached for her mother and grandmother.

Even this Christmas.

The light filtering beneath her curtains dimmed for a moment when she slid her hands over her stomach. She dragged in a breath, sat up, and threw back the covers. No moping today. Today was for Jason and Luke. She wanted them to experience just a little Christmas magic—to realise that they shouldn't shut themselves off from the joy the day had to offer.

Shouldn't shut themselves off from any of the joys the world had to offer.

She tiptoed through the house, careful not to wake anyone. She needn't have bothered. She found Luke and Jason at the kitchen table, eating fruitcake.

'Ooh, fruitcake for breakfast! Excellent idea. Merry Christmas, Luke. Merry Christmas, Jason.'

'Merry Christmas, Keira.' Luke leapt up to pour her a

coffee. He looked so fresh and bright and eager her heart expanded.

'Merry Christmas, Keira.' Jason cut her a slice of fruitcake, his grin wide and his eyes thrilling with the same excitement that rippled through her.

It took her precisely half a cup of coffee and two generous bites of fruitcake before she realised Jason and Luke had no idea how to proceed with the day. A wave of tenderness engulfed her. Across in the living room, early-morning sun poured in at the windows and the French doors, winking off tinsel and angel chains and Christmas lanterns. She nodded. 'It looks like fairyland in there.'

'I'm going to be vacuuming tinsel up for the next six months,' Luke grumbled.

But his eyes twinkled and Keira grinned at him. 'Every time you come across another piece you're going to remember what a marvellous Christmas you had,' she countered. 'C'mon.' She stood. 'I've never been able to show the least restraint on Christmas morning.'

She set a tray of mini-croissants into the oven, and then tripped into the living room. 'It has to be present-opening time!'

At different stages on the previous day, unseen by the others, each of them had tiptoed into the living room to put presents beneath the Christmas tree. It made it seem as if those presents had appeared by magic, even though she knew they hadn't. She clasped her hands beneath her chin. 'It almost looks too pretty to disturb.'

Jason groaned.

'That's what my mother would say every year,' she said with a laugh. 'And I'd always point out that she'd said *almost*… and that I harboured no such scruple.'

She settled on the carpet in front of the tree and rifled through the presents. 'Here—catch!' She tossed identical packages to Luke and Jason.

They stared at the presents in awe, and then glanced around as if figuring what they should do next. Keira shuffled along a bit, and with shrugs they settled themselves on the floor to form an arc around the Christmas tree with her.

Keira. Jason. Luke.

She tried not to notice how perfect that seemed.

A bark of laughter shot out of Luke when he tore his present open to discover the chunky three-pack of sports socks and the outrageously loud satin boxers encased within.

Jason sniggered. 'Going to model them?' Then promptly closed his mouth when he realised that his was an identical gift.

Luke leant over and placed a brightly wrapped present in front of her. She tore the package open with more speed than grace—vanilla-scented shower gel, body lotion and bath bombs! She clapped her hands and suspected her grin threatened to take over her entire face. 'You've got the hang of this, Hillier.'

'My turn!' Jason said.

His gift to her was a book of nonsense verse that made them all laugh. His gift to his father was a DVD box set of action movies, and an accompanying movie directory book.

'I've been wanting to see this movie for ages!' Luke selected one from the box and glanced at the television.

'Later,' Jason decreed, leaping up to put the Christmas CD on. When he opened his present from his father, though—the dragon game—he gazed longingly at his game console.

In unison, Keira and Luke said, 'Later!'

Keira knew Christmas wasn't about presents, but Luke and Jason hadn't had presents in three years. And to see the happiness that the presents they'd selected could bring to someone's face…and to be made to feel special by someone else's carefully selected presents…that was priceless.

As unobtrusively as she could, she retrieved the croissants and made a fresh pot of coffee, and brought the tray through to the living room. She set her other presents in front of Luke and Jason.

'Sweet!' Jason immediately immersed himself in the Manga comics she'd selected for him.

Luke's eyes darkened when he unwrapped his gift—a leather wallet with a snakeskin design. All she'd written on the tag was 'My Hero!'

When his eyes met hers she knew he remembered that day down by the river as vividly as she did. 'Merry Christmas, Luke.' Her voice came out husky, but she found she could do absolutely nothing about that.

He leant across and placed the last remaining present in her lap. 'Merry Christmas, Keira.'

She tore open the paper and laughed as she drew out a hot-pink sun hat, but nestled in its crown was a silk scarf in all the colours of the rainbow—orange bleeding into yellow and green, then violet and finally cobalt blue. 'I don't think I've ever owned anything so beautiful.'

She promptly settled the hat on her head, and wound the scarf around her throat. Jason pronounced it, 'fully sweet'.

Luke leant over to finger the delicate silk. 'It suits you.'

Her heart billowed and skipped.

They all stretched out—Jason on the floor, Luke in his armchair, her on the sofa—and munched croissants and drank coffee, becoming immersed in their books and comics. Occasionally one of them would read something out to the others.

Keira glanced surreptitiously around. This was perfect. It hit her then, with a clarity she could no longer ignore or deny—this was what she wanted. This was where she wanted to be for the rest of her life.

With one final glance at Luke, she closed her eyes and prayed again for a Christmas miracle.

* * *

Luke started when Keira leapt up with a squeak. 'It's time we got the turkey on!'

Jason scrambled to his feet. 'You said you'd show me what to do.'

'I will indeed.'

Luke pushed out of his chair more slowly, found a piece of gift paper to use as a bookmark in his movie directory book, amazed at how much he'd lost himself in the ease of the morning.

Keira and Jason's wide eyes and laughter during their exchange of gifts had told him that the whole Christmas thing was working. What he hadn't expected was that it would work its magic on him too.

Keira was right. There *was* a magic to Christmas. He moved towards the kitchen for potato-peeling duty, determined that she wouldn't be stuck with all the hard work. He couldn't remember the last time his shoulders had swung so loose and free.

'That's all there is to it?' Luke asked, stunned, when Keira set the turkey and vegetables in the oven.

She dusted off her hands. 'We put the sprouts on and make the gravy a little before we're ready to eat. And the turkey will need basting every now and again.'

'I'll do that,' Jason volunteered. 'You showed me what to do.'

She shrugged. 'So, yes, that's pretty much all there is to it.'

'I should be able to manage that on my own next year.'

At his words, he could have sworn her smile slipped, but it emerged with renewed vigour and he figured he must have imagined it. 'That's the plan.'

She wanted to set him up for all future Christmases—Christmases when she wouldn't be here. A rock lodged in his chest. Would he have the heart to celebrate Christmas next year?

He glanced at Jason and pulled his shoulders back. He'd celebrate next year if for no other reason than for his son. He would not let things slide so badly ever again. That was Keira's true gift to him.

If only he could give her something so precious.

His mind suddenly whirred and clicked. Maybe he could?

'C'mon, Jason. I'm dying to check out this game of yours.'

With a whoop, Jason shot into the living room. Keira stopped by Luke, touched his arm. 'Are you okay?'

He gestured towards Jason. 'Thank you. It's been a perfect day so far.'

'Yeah, it has.' She dimpled up at him, and all he could think about was kissing her. 'But the fun's not over yet. C'mon.'

He followed her, but kept at least three feet between them as they made their way back into the living room. It would be too dangerous to get caught under the mistletoe with her today. Christmas might contain a spark of magic, but it couldn't change the past. Nor could it change the future he'd set out before him.

Christmas dinner lived up to expectation. They all ate too much, and it all tasted so good that Luke wanted to keep eating—only he couldn't fit another morsel in.

After lunch Keira made them play charades and other party games. Luke lost every time. He'd find himself caught up in the way her hair bounced, fascinated by the mobility of her features.

He didn't enjoy himself any the less for that.

When the phone rang and no one else moved to answer it, Luke lumbered to his feet. He pressed the receiver to his ear. 'Hello?'

A tiny pause, then, 'Luke…hello.'

Brenda! Heaviness slammed into him. Guilt that he hadn't given Brenda and Alf a second thought so far today. Guilt that he was alive and healthy when Tammy was not. 'I…uh…I guess you'd like to speak to Jason. I'll get him for you.'

'Thank you. And Luke…?'

He paused in the act of gesturing to his son, and braced himself for something hard and crushing.

'Merry Christmas.'

He stared at the receiver. He couldn't have heard that correctly. He pressed it against his ear again. Swallowed. 'Merry Christmas to you and Alf too, Brenda.'

'Thank you.'

Without another word, he handed the phone to Jason. Dazed, he moved back to his chair.

Keira touched his knee. 'Is everything okay?'

'Brenda…she just wished me a merry Christmas.' He still couldn't believe he'd heard that right.

Keira's smile when it came wasn't one of those big ones that could dazzle and unbalance a man. It was both softer and deeper, and more devastating, than that. 'A Christmas miracle,' she whispered.

He didn't believe in miracles, but…

'Dad?' Luke turned to find Jason holding the phone against his chest. 'Is it okay if I spend tonight with Gran and Grandad?'

Luke nodded, and waited for Jason to call him back to the phone so Brenda could retract her merry Christmas.

Jason spoke a few more words into the phone, and then settled it back into its cradle before flopping onto the sofa. 'It's all good. They're going to collect me later this afternoon.'

'Sorted?' Keira asked.

'Sorted,' Jason said. 'Gran almost sounded like her old self again.'

Luke blinked. A Christmas miracle?

'This has been the sweetest Christmas ever.'

Luke couldn't argue with that.

Jason's grandparents collected him at four p.m. They didn't come in, but they waved from the car. Luke hugged his son, ordered him to have a good time, and waved back.

The car drove away and Luke dragged in a breath and braced his shoulders. There was only one more thing he wanted to accomplish today...

'Tired?' he asked Keira when he returned. She was curled up on the sofa, her head propped up on one hand. She'd remained inside while he said farewell to Jason. Diplomacy, he suspected. She hadn't wanted to remind Brenda and Alf of Tammy.

Not that he and Keira had that kind of relationship. He rolled his shoulders. They did have a friendship, though.

'Pleasantly so,' she said.

'Are you up to sharing a bottle of wine on the veranda? I have a bottle of Pinot Gris here that should be as smooth and mellow as anything you've ever tasted.'

'Ooh, yes, please!' She swung around to stare at him. 'That sounds *divine*.'

He grabbed the bottle and two wine glasses and led the way out to the veranda and around to the bench at the side. This spot was one of his favourite places in the world.

Keira leant against the veranda railing. 'You were right, you know, Luke. This view really is wonderful. It'd be worth quite a bit of inconvenience for the privilege of waking up to it every day.'

'So you're not sorry fate sent you here to Candlebark?'

She settled herself on the bench. The scent of vanilla rose up around him, mingling with the bouquet of the wine. She took the glass he handed her. He was careful their fingers didn't touch.

'I'm not the least sorry that I landed at Candlebark. Meeting you and Jason—that's been quite an adventure.'

'Have you had a nice day today?'

'Yes…and I didn't really expect to. I just wanted to try to make it nice for you and Jason, but…well, somehow I got swept up in it too.'

'That makes the two of us.'

He stared at her for a long moment, prayed that what he was about to do was the right thing. His gut told him it was.

She touched a hand to her face. 'What?'

He shook himself. Made himself stare out at the golden expanse of wheat. 'You've given me a lot of good advice over these last two weeks, Keira—about Jason, about myself, about Christmas. It appears you were even right about Brenda and Alf. I can't begin to thank you.'

She half-grimaced, half-grinned. 'Considering most of that advice was unsolicited, Luke, I don't think you need to thank me.'

He stared at her steadily for another long moment. 'I want to offer some unsolicited advice in return.'

Luke's eyes were gentle, and that particular shade of rich golden-brown that could make her mouth water. She swallowed. He stared at her as if he cared about her.

Of course he cares about you. As a friend.

She drew her bottom lip into her mouth. His eyes fastened on that action, darkened. Her blood quickened. Her heart skipped. Was it possible that she could get her Christmas miracle after all?

'Advice?' she whispered. She couldn't do anything about the huskiness that had invaded her voice, or the yearning that invaded her soul.

'I think you should continue to pursue your IVF treatment.'

She settled her wine glass on the floorboards at her feet, turned to stare out at all that golden wheat, rippling like a promise across the landscape, and waited for the darkness, the emptiness, to claim her.

A heavy sadness pressed against her heart, and tiredness made her want to rest her head against the wall behind, but the darkness didn't settle over her to block out the sun or the glory of the view or the presence of the man sitting next her.

She blinked and risked a deep breath. The darkness remained at bay.

And then a new thought banished her tiredness. 'It seems to matter to you.'

'Of course it matters!' He stared at her as if she'd gone mad. 'This is important.' He reached out and took her hand. 'You helped me rediscover the joys of fatherhood. And believe me, it *is* a joy. I want that for you. I want you to experience that blessing. You deserve it.'

Because he cared about her?

'You'll make a great mum, Keira.'

She left her hand in his because it felt so right. 'Luke, in the last fortnight I've learned a lot about myself. You showed me how counterproductive it's been to try and follow in my mother and grandmother's footsteps, that I've perhaps mistaken strength for necessity, and for putting a good and brave face on a less than ideal situation. I've finally acknowledged to myself something I've always been too scared to admit before.'

He leaned towards her, eyes intent.

She wanted to take his face in her hands and kiss him. She resisted the impulse. There was too much to say first. 'I don't want to be a single parent. I don't want to have to do it all on my own. If I had another miscarriage…' She shook her head. 'I don't know how I would get through that.'

He opened his mouth, but she shook her head again and held up her free hand. 'I know you're going to say my friends would help me through it, and of course they would. But it's not the same as having someone by my side who'd hoped for the baby and loved it as much as I did.'

Luke stared out at the view, but Keira wasn't sure how much of it he saw. Those grooves bit deep either side of his mouth. Grief for her and her baby? The thought made her throat thicken.

'Yes, I want a baby...babies if at all possible. But not at the expense of everything else. I have to decide if I really am prepared to do it on my own, or whether to take my chances and wait. That's not a decision I can come to in a couple of days.'

He turned and nodded.

She smiled, desperately wanting him to smile back. 'I appreciate your concern, though.'

She squeezed his hand and prayed as hard as she could for her Christmas miracle. Luke's eyes had gone gentle again, but...

But nothing. He didn't lean forward to kiss her. He didn't open his mouth to tell her he cared for her, that he wanted to keep seeing her or...anything.

A faint heart never won a fat duck.

She blinked as those words sounded through her mind. It had been one of her grandmother's favourite sayings.

It hit her then. True strength lay in going after what she wanted rather than hoping it would come to her in some magical way...waiting and hoping because she was too scared to reach out and take it for herself, too scared to open herself up and be vulnerable.

She moistened her lips and swallowed. Did she dare?

Her heart pounded so loud she could hardly believe Luke couldn't hear it. 'Luke, if I wasn't leaving next week I wouldn't mention this now, but...'

'But?'

She straightened and met his gaze head-on. 'I...Luke, I love you.'

His head snapped back. She didn't know what that meant or how to read it. She swallowed and refused to allow herself the luxury of a retreat. Her grandmother had been right. *A faint heart never won a fat duck.* 'I didn't plan on this happening—not in a million years—but I think you care about me a little… and I was wondering if perhaps we might be able to keep seeing each other and see where it might all lead to?'

Her words faltered to a halt. He'd reefed his hand from hers and she knew precisely how to read that. She gripped her hands together to stop their shaking, but there was nothing she could do to prevent her heart from shattering.

Luke jerked to his feet, banging his hip hard against the arm of the bench in his haste to move away from her and all her glorious sweetness and warmth. He set his wine glass down, wiped away the wetness that had spilled across his hand.

She was handing him everything he'd ever wanted. No—more than that. Because she was more than he could ever have imagined. But he couldn't accept it.

What he felt for Keira—it wouldn't last. He had a false heart. If he hadn't been able to give Tammy what she'd need-ed—the woman who'd meant most to him in the world—then he couldn't be trusted with a woman's heart at all. End of story. He would break it—break her.

His chest constricted so painfully he couldn't breathe. He couldn't do that to Keira!

As she stared at him, tears caught on the ends of her eyelashes and hung there like stars. The stars spilled from her lashes and trailed down her cheeks to the corners of her mouth. He wanted to reach out and catch them before they were gone for ever. But he could only do that if he gave her what she asked for.

Air rushed back into his lungs. He clenched his hands together to keep them at his sides. 'I'm sorry, Keira. I can't give you what you want or what you need.' No matter how much he wanted to. All he could give her was potential heartache and disappointment.

Keira dashed her tears away, folded her arms and hitched up her chin. 'Why not? I know you care about me.'

Yeah, he did. But how would she cope when he let her down the way he'd let Tammy down? He couldn't risk it.

Her chin wobbled. 'Why won't you take a risk on us?'

He didn't want to talk about this, but she'd laid her heart on the line with total honesty. If she saw him for what he really was...

Sourness filled his mouth. Her happiness mattered more than what she thought of him. 'Keira, my first marriage was hell. I didn't love Tammy.'

She didn't back away. Her eyes didn't widen in horror.

'No marriage can be happy with that knowledge pulsing in the silences.' At eighteen, he'd had a crush on Tammy. When she'd fallen pregnant he'd done the right thing and married her. But then Tammy had discovered the truth—the fickleness of his feelings. He hadn't even been able to pretend. People stayed together for their children's sakes, but he hadn't even been able to manage that much.

'Tammy knew?'

'Not at first.' He forced himself to say the words out loud. 'But when she found out it broke her heart.'

'Oh, Luke.' Her eyes turned dove-grey. 'So that's where all this guilt comes from. This is why you punish yourself.'

She knew how badly he'd failed Tammy, and yet she was still standing here. Didn't she know—?

'You told me you never cheated on Tammy, or made her feel guilty for falling pregnant, and that you weren't cruel to her.' She took a step towards him. 'You can't keep punishing yourself like this.'

He dropped back to the bench, head in his hands, and tried to beat back the darkness. She perched beside him. She didn't touch him, but the scent of vanilla drifted around him, torturing him with its sweetness.

'You don't get it. I told her I loved her. I thought I did.' If only he could relive that day, spare her. 'And we...' He lifted his head. 'I was her first and...'

'And then Jason happened?'

He nodded heavily. 'She gave up all her dreams to have him.'

'No, she didn't. You took her to the city, didn't you?'

He dragged a hand down his face. 'That didn't make up for lying to her!'

'You didn't know it was a lie at the time.'

He straightened. The pain pierced his very core. 'You didn't see her face when she demanded to know the truth—did I love her or not?' Tammy had known him so well. His hands clenched. 'It was like...the lights went out.'

Keira's eyes filled with tears. For his dead wife? 'I'm sorry,' she whispered. 'You didn't mean to hurt her.'

'Do you think that's any consolation?' The words broke from him, harsh and loud. 'I loved my home more than the woman I married. I chose *this*—' he flung an arm out '—over her. What kind of man does that make me?'

'Oh, Luke.'

No! He didn't want her sympathy. He didn't deserve it. The vision of Tammy's stricken face, her tear-swollen eyes, filled his mind. Her mute pain. Her guilt. *Her guilt!*

He gave a harsh laugh, leapt to his feet. He'd betrayed her—his best friend. He'd have laid his life down for her in an instant, but he hadn't been able to do the one thing that would have made a difference—love her the way she'd loved him.

And then she'd died and...and the despair...

And the release.

He hated himself for it.

'I don't deserve a second chance, Keira. I'm sorry, but I

can't be what you want me to be. I might love you now, but in the end I'll do to you what I did to Tammy.'

'You can't know that!'

He remained silent. There was nothing left to say.

'And the fact that I love you and that you care about me—that doesn't make any difference?'

The panic that raced across her face snagged at his heart. He couldn't let it make a difference. 'I can't be trusted.' He had to protect her.

She shot to her feet, stabbed a finger at him. 'You think you know what's best for everyone, but you're wrong!' Her finger shook. 'You'll sacrifice your happiness and mine to that belief because you're an emotional coward who doesn't have the gumption to take a risk!' She flung an arm out, swung away only to swing back again. 'How *dare* you preach to me about going after my dream of motherhood when you refuse to even dream at all?'

She dragged in a breath, and he could almost see her count to three. She took a step away from him. 'It's been a big day. I'm tired. I'm going to take a nap. There are a lot of leftovers. I propose that if we get hungry later we just make ourselves up a plate.'

With that, she turned and left. Luke realised she'd just become the lodger he'd so desperately wanted two weeks ago. And now—now all he wanted was the warm, vibrant woman that was Keira.

CHAPTER TWELVE

LUKE paced the edge of the crowd, astounded at the number of people who had shown up for the auction. Keira's estate agent had drummed up an enormous amount of interest in record time.

He wished he could feel more impressed about that.

He glanced at Keira's great-aunt's house—Keira's house— and a rock settled in his chest. She should have had the chance to live and work there, to have her baby and run her physio-therapy clinic and be surrounded by a community who would have embraced her.

His fists clenched. It should have all been hers!

It still could be.

He pushed that insidious thought away. He couldn't give her what she needed.

And he wasn't an emotional coward. He was trying to protect her!

He glanced at the house again and the rock grew. He glanced over at Keira, who was talking to the estate agent, and the rock developed jagged edges. He'd wanted to bring her to the auction today, but she'd refused to let him. She'd packed up her car, intent on returning to Sydney as soon as the auction was over. He should be out in that boundary paddock of his, demolishing weeds.

He hadn't been able to stay away.

Her red-gold hair gleamed in the sunshine. Darn it, she

wasn't wearing a hat. If she weren't careful she'd burn to a crisp.

You'll sacrifice your happiness and mine.

His happiness didn't matter, and he wasn't sacrificing hers. She'd find someone new, someone worthy of her love, and—

His thought processes stumbled to a halt. He rewound his previous thought, went back over it carefully to test its truth, its validity. Did he seriously mean that—that her happiness was more important than his?

His mouth went dry. If his happiness didn't matter... then...

His head reared back. What a blind fool he'd been! His feelings for Keira were so far beyond what he'd ever felt for any other woman as to be laughable. He'd do anything to give her what she wanted, what she needed. He'd make any sacrifice...

Including Candlebark.

He swore—low and swift—as he tried to counter the panic racing through him. Had he left it too late? Through the crowd he identified the grey hair and sloping shoulders of his bank manager. Without further ado he shouldered his way through the crowd towards him.

'I mean to bid and I mean to win,' he said without preamble. 'Will you stake me a bridging loan until I can sell Candlebark?'

The bank manager was clearly stunned. 'Are you sure?'

'Yes.'

Luke held out his hand. The other man shook it. 'Done.'

Once the bidding on Great-Aunt Ada's house had started, Keira couldn't look at the crowd. She didn't have the heart for it.

She knew Luke was in that crowd somewhere. She'd sensed

him there earlier, before the auction had started. She hadn't needed to turn around to confirm it, but she had anyway.

He'd stood tall and grim on the outskirts of the crowd, his lips tight and those grooves biting deep into the flesh on either side of his mouth. She'd swung away again, before he caught her staring.

What was he doing here?

Her lips twisted. Maybe he wanted to make sure she really did leave town, and that she no longer meant to trespass on his hospitality?

He need have no worries on that score. She'd made enough of a fool of herself over him already. She was in no hurry to repeat the performance. A girl had to have some pride. She'd be driving away from here some time in the next hour and she would *never* return.

But the thought shrivelled her heart up as hard and tight as a walnut.

Pride be damned! She'd beg him to give their love a chance if she thought it would make a difference.

Only it wouldn't.

All she could do now was studiously avert her gaze from the crowd—from Luke—and try with all her might to stop from falling apart in public. Problem was, that only left her one place to look—at Great-Aunt Ada's lovely colonial-style cottage. A reminder of the dreams that had taken seed there burned and prickled through her. As did the guilt that she was selling off part of her heritage.

She clenched her hands together and did her best to block the rapid-fire bidding from her ears. She didn't have any other options. She couldn't stay in Gunnedah. Living in the same town as the man she'd fallen in love with was not a sure-fire method of getting over him, of that she was certain. And she wasn't a masochist.

'Excellent,' Julia murmured in Keira's ear, tapping her

clipboard. 'We've reached the reserve price. Your house is now officially on the market. It will be sold today.'

Keira's eyes burned. She gripped her hands tighter.

'I don't know what's got into Luke Hillier, though,' Julia continued. 'He's bidding like a man possessed.'

The iron-bar rigidity left her body on one big out breath.

'What?' She spun around.

To discover Julia was in earnest.

Luke was bidding on her house!

What on earth...?

'Will you excuse me for a moment?'

Not waiting for Julia's reply, Keira threaded her way through the sea of bodies to where Luke stood. 'What on earth do you think you're doing?' she ground out as quietly as she could. She wanted to scream!

'Buying your house.' He spoke just as low, and then raised his hand to indicate another bid.

She grabbed it and hauled it back down. 'But... But...you can't afford it.'

'Yes, he can,' said the man standing beside Luke.

He handed her a business card. Luke's bank manager? But... Her brain wouldn't work.

One thing she did know. 'I am *not* selling my house to you,' she hissed.

'Listen here—' the bank manager pitched his voice low '—Luke's money is as good as anyone else's, missy.'

Keira gave up all pretence at discretion. 'What did you just call me? Missy? *Missy!* What kind of Neanderthal—?'

'Uh, Keira...'

Luke touched her arm. She glanced up to find everyone had turned to stare. Anger that she wanted Luke to not only keep touching her but to haul her into his arms overrode her embarrassment.

She focused on the anger, not the despair. 'Why on earth would *you* want to buy *my* house?'

She suspected she might well die a thousand deaths over making such a public display when she went back over this scene later. In fact, this was proof positive that she wasn't quite over making a fool of herself where this man was concerned after all, wasn't it?

Her chin shot up. What did it matter? She'd be leaving here in an hour, and these people would never see her again. What did it matter what they thought of her?

'How on earth can you afford it?' she demanded. 'Not by renting out that Spartan room of yours—of that I'm certain!'

He shuffled his feet and glanced around. Keira did too. The auction proceedings had ground to a categorical standstill. She gritted her teeth and reminded herself that she didn't care what these people thought of her.

Amazingly, when Luke's gaze returned to her, his lips twitched. 'I'm guessing you're not going to wait till the auction is over for an explanation?'

She shook her head. 'Not a chance.'

'I can afford to buy your house if I sell Candlebark. It's that's simple.'

She gaped at him. He couldn't sell his home. He loved it! It was a part of him. Why would he even *consider* such a thing?

He continued to survey her with that curious half-smile and her mouth went dry. 'Why would you do that?' she croaked.

'Because I was wrong.'

Her heart stuttered and threatened to take flight. She tried to rein it in. She planted her hands on her hips. 'About which bit, precisely?'

He didn't hesitate. 'The bit about not being able to give you what you needed.' His chin jutted out. He planted his feet. 'I know I've been blind…an idiot…but just give me a chance to prove myself to you, Keira, and I will.'

She had no hope of restraining the wild hope that gripped her.

'I know you dreamed of raising children here in your great-aunt's house, of establishing your physiotherapy practice and being part of a community. You deserve to have all those things, and they can still be yours. I *can* be the husband you need. I *can* be the father of your children.' He hauled in a breath. 'If that's what you still want, that is. If I haven't left it too late.'

He was prepared to sell his farm to give her what he thought she most wanted in life? Her throat grew so thick she couldn't so much as utter one word.

'What you want and what you need are more important than where I live or what kind of job I have or…or anything. I want to spend my life with you—whether that's here in your aunt's house or in the city. Keira—' he reached out and gripped her hands '—I love you.'

She couldn't help it. Her heart burst free with all its hope and joy. She threw herself at him and wound her arms around his neck. All around them cheers and applause broke out. 'You idiot,' she whispered, resting her forehead against his. 'I don't need you to sell Candlebark to prove that to me.'

'Sweetheart, after everything I've put you through I can't expect you to take me on trust.'

She drew back to gaze into his face. 'Why not?'

His eyes widened.

She threw her head back and laughed for the sheer joy of it. 'Luke, wherever you are, that's my home. All the other bits don't matter. Please don't sell Candlebark. I would love to raise our children there. My great-aunt's house will make the perfect clinic—just like we said.'

'Are you sure?' He cupped her face in his hands. 'I want you to know that I would give it up in an instant for you.'

She knew he meant it. And she knew what he was trying to tell her. She wondered if it were possible to melt from sheer happiness. 'I'm positive, Luke. Now...' She cocked what she hoped was a cheeky eyebrow, but her heart pounded in her chest so loudly everyone within a two-metre radius must hear it. 'You said something about being the husband that I needed. Was that a proposal of marriage?'

His eyes darkened. 'Yes, it was. But it was a darn clumsy one.'

He went down on one knee in front of what felt like the whole town. Heat surged into her cheeks, but whether from embarrassment or happiness she couldn't tell. 'Keira, will you do me the very great honour of making me the happiest man on the planet and becoming my wife?'

'Yes,' she said simply, pulling him back to his feet. 'Now, kiss me.'

And he did.

Then it seemed everyone was crowding around them to shake Luke's hand and to kiss her cheek and to offer congratulations.

Julia bustled up. 'Do I take it that the house is off the market?'

'Oh, yes!' Keira seized the other woman's arm. 'Julia, I'm so sorry. I've put you to an awful lot of trouble for no reason.'

'Not at all,' the agent said with a laugh, patting Keira's hand. 'I wouldn't have missed this for the world. Congratulations to both of you. I don't doubt that once word gets out our next auction will be packed to the rafters.'

'I do hope so!'

Before she could say anything more Jason came racing up, his grin wide. With a whoop, he picked Keira up and swung her around. 'That was fully sweet, Dad!' He put her down to clap his father on the shoulder.

That was when Keira saw Brenda, standing on the fringes of the crowd. She hesitated for a moment, before moving towards the older woman and taking her hand. 'That must've been terribly difficult for you to witness.'

Brenda squeezed her hand. 'It wasn't as bad as I thought it would be.'

Keira led her across the road to a park bench. 'Are you okay?'

Brenda sat. 'I think so.'

Keira sat too. She stared at the sky, at the house opposite, at the crowd. 'I don't know if this is common knowledge yet or not. I don't know how quickly news spreads in a country town...but a couple of weeks ago I had a miscarriage.' She paused. Stared at the sky again. 'I wanted that baby so much... and then I had the miscarriage...'

She let the words trail off. She knew Brenda would understand. 'But I never held my child in my arms. I never waved her off on her first day of school, waited in the emergency room while she had a broken arm set, watched her grow up and blossom into a woman with a child of her own. I can't begin to know how terrible and difficult your grief must be, Brenda.'

'And yet,' Brenda said slowly, 'we had our Tammy to love for thirty years.' She stared down at her hands. 'Jason was right. I've let my bitterness twist me. I wanted to blame someone and I fixed on poor Luke. I know what happened wasn't his fault.' She lifted her head and met Keira's gaze. 'The thing is, while I've missed Tammy more than I can say, I've missed Luke too. He and Tammy were thick as thieves when they were growing up. He spent as much time at our place as he did at his own. He was always like a son to me.'

Keira swallowed and moistened her lips. 'So...you wish him well?'

'I hope the two of you will be very happy, Keira.'

Keira's heart soared. 'And will you and Alf come to our wedding?'

'We'd be delighted to.'

'And dinner next week?'

'That would be lovely.'

Both women stood as Luke made his way across to them. Brenda reached up and kissed Luke's cheek. 'Congratulations, Luke.'

'Thank you.'

'Now I must be off, to tell Alfred the news.'

'I'll call you,' Keira said.

'You do that, dear.'

Luke's jaw dropped. Keira reached up and tapped it closed. He swung to her. 'I swear, woman, you're a witch!'

She shrugged. 'I didn't do anything.'

One corner of his mouth hooked up. 'How can you say that when you've waltzed into town and turned my life upside down?' He collapsed onto the bench and then reached out to seize her around her waist and drag her down into his lap. 'How can you say that when you've bewitched me body and soul until I can think of nothing but you?'

'Oh, Luke.' She laid her hand against his cheek. 'Are you happy? Really? Is this really what you want?'

'With my whole heart,' he vowed. 'What I feel for you, Keira, is a man's love. It's deep and true...' his eyes darkened '...and unchangeable. What I felt for Tammy was a boy's crush mixed up with friendship. It's taken me a long time to realise the difference. I couldn't stand the thought of hurting you the way I'd hurt her.'

He stared out to the front, his mouth tight for a moment. 'It wasn't until the auction was about to start that I realised I'd give up everything—including Candlebark—if only you could have what you wanted. When I realised I'd choose you over my home, my livelihood, my way of life. That's when I knew what I felt for you was something different—something I'd never experienced before. And I hoped I hadn't left it too late to tell you that.'

Keira stared at him in awe for a moment. Then she smiled.

'You didn't leave it too late, Luke. You timed it perfectly. I got my Christmas miracle after all.'

He traced her cheek with one long, tanned finger. '*You* are my Christmas miracle, Keira.'

Her heart swelled so big she could hardly breathe. 'I love you, Luke.'

'And I love you. I mean to spend a lifetime showing you just how much.'

She cocked that cheeky eyebrow again. 'You could always start right now, by kissing me.'

His grin when it came was low and sexy. 'What an excellent idea.'

MILLS & BOON®

DECEMBER 2010 HARDBACK TITLES

ROMANCE

Naive Bride, Defiant Wife	Lynne Graham
Nicolo: The Powerful Sicilian	Sandra Marton
Stranded, Seduced...Pregnant	Kim Lawrence
Shock: One-Night Heir	Melanie Milburne
Innocent Virgin, Wild Surrender	Anne Mather
Her Last Night of Innocence	India Grey
Captured and Crowned	Janette Kenny
Buttoned-Up Secretary, British Boss	Susanne James
Surf, Sea and a Sexy Stranger	Heidi Rice
Wild Nights with her Wicked Boss	Nicola Marsh
Mistletoe and the Lost Stiletto	Liz Fielding
Rescued by his Christmas Angel	Cara Colter
Angel of Smoky Hollow	Barbara McMahon
Christmas at Candlebark Farm	Michelle Douglas
The Cinderella Bride	Barbara Wallace
Single Father, Surprise Prince!	Raye Morgan
A Christmas Knight	Kate Hardy
The Nurse Who Saved Christmas	Janice Lynn

HISTORICAL

Lady Arabella's Scandalous Marriage	Carole Mortimer
Dangerous Lord, Seductive Miss	Mary Brendan
Bound to the Barbarian	Carol Townend
Bought: The Penniless Lady	Deborah Hale

MEDICAL™

St Piran's: The Wedding of The Year	Caroline Anderson
St Piran's: Rescuing Pregnant Cinderella	Carol Marinelli
The Midwife's Christmas Miracle	Jennifer Taylor
The Doctor's Society Sweetheart	Lucy Clark

MILLS & BOON®

DECEMBER 2010 LARGE PRINT TITLES

ROMANCE

The Pregnancy Shock	Lynne Graham
Falco: The Dark Guardian	Sandra Marton
One Night...Nine-Month Scandal	Sarah Morgan
The Last Kolovsky Playboy	Carol Marinelli
Doorstep Twins	Rebecca Winters
The Cowboy's Adopted Daughter	Patricia Thayer
SOS: Convenient Husband Required	Liz Fielding
Winning a Groom in 10 Dates	Cara Colter

HISTORICAL

Rake Beyond Redemption	Anne O'Brien
A Thoroughly Compromised Lady	Bronwyn Scott
In the Master's Bed	Blythe Gifford
Bought: The Penniless Lady	Deborah Hale

MEDICAL™

The Midwife and the Millionaire	Fiona McArthur
From Single Mum to Lady	Judy Campbell
Knight on the Children's Ward	Carol Marinelli
Children's Doctor, Shy Nurse	Molly Evans
Hawaiian Sunset, Dream Proposal	Joanna Neil
Rescued: Mother and Baby	Anne Fraser

JANUARY 2011 HARDBACK TITLES

ROMANCE

Hidden Mistress, Public Wife	Emma Darcy
Jordan St Claire: Dark and Dangerous	Carole Mortimer
The Forbidden Innocent	Sharon Kendrick
Bound to the Greek	Kate Hewitt
The Secretary's Scandalous Secret	Cathy Williams
Ruthless Boss, Dream Baby	Susan Stephens
Prince Voronov's Virgin	Lynn Raye Harris
Mistress, Mother...Wife?	Maggie Cox
With This Fling...	Kelly Hunter
Girls' Guide to Flirting with Danger	Kimberly Lang
Wealthy Australian, Secret Son	Margaret Way
A Winter Proposal	Lucy Gordon
His Diamond Bride	Lucy Gordon
Surprise: Outback Proposal	Jennie Adams
Juggling Briefcase & Baby	Jessica Hart
Deserted Island, Dreamy Ex!	Nicola Marsh
Rescued by the Dreamy Doc	Amy Andrews
Navy Officer to Family Man	Emily Forbes

HISTORICAL

Lady Folbroke's Delicious Deception	Christine Merrill
Breaking the Governess's Rules	Michelle Styles
Her Dark and Dangerous Lord	Anne Herries
How To Marry a Rake	Deb Marlowe

MEDICAL™

Sheikh, Children's Doctor...Husband	Meredith Webber
Six-Week Marriage Miracle	Jessica Matthews
St Piran's: Italian Surgeon, Forbidden Bride	Margaret McDonagh
The Baby Who Stole the Doctor's Heart	Dianne Drake

1210 Gen Std LP

MILLS & BOON®

JANUARY 2011 LARGE PRINT TITLES

ROMANCE

HISTORICAL

MEDICAL™